Daughter of Bones

by

Grace Colline

Cover Art by *The Wild Rose Press, Inc.*

The Wild Rose Press, Inc.
PO Box 708
Adams Basin, NY 14410-0708
Visit us at www.thewildrosepress.com

Publishing History
First Edition, 2025
Trade Paperback ISBN 978-1-5092-5961-8
Digital ISBN 978-1-5092-5962-5

Published in the United States of America

Author's Note

From 1877-1892, in the rich bone beds of Colorado, Wyoming, and Nebraska, two paleontologists fought it out for control of the best dinosaur bones. Othniel Marsh, and Edward Cope were two of the preeminent researchers of their time. Once friends, they had become bitter rivals and often stooped to spying and even sabotage in their efforts to destroy the other's finds.

Smaller paleontologists would find themselves pressured into surrendering their finds to one or the other as the two often raced to describe new species and attack each other in scientific publications.

Given the rather lawless nature of the west at this time, it is not surprising that dinosaur hunting became a dangerous past-time. In this background, many dramas were played out and stories born.

This is one of them.

Chapter One

Matson, Colorado, Spring 1879

Shadows spread across the table, forcing Elizabeth Ingram to squint. The tray of sand shifted as she pushed back a little, then rubbed her eyes. Sighing heavily, she lifted the skull and peered closely at the point where it emerged from the solid rock matrix around it. The smooth cream of the bone was in sharp contrast with the reddish stone, making this an easier piece to work on.

She set it down in the tray, covered it with the linen cloth and set the fine metal pick and the paintbrush down next to it. Switching her skirt out of the way, she stood and stretched for a moment, then made her way out of the preparation room and into the busy jumble of her father's office in the little museum.

Books and papers lay scattered across the large desk, which consisted of an old door set across a pair of trestles. It had a tendency to collapse and so was reinforced by a pile of books at both ends. She had once rearranged the museum's budget to squeeze some money out to be able to purchase him a solid, second-hand, desk. Instead, he had taken the money and invested it in another dig, and she had conceded defeat. Things simply did not matter to Dr. Wilberforce Ingram, only the bones.

Bones. Elizabeth looked through the open doorway to the dark museum beyond. She had never known anything different than the Fossil Emporium her father had established when she was a little girl. Her education had consisted of her mother teaching her how to read and write and do arithmetic, and her father teaching her a humerus from a femur, and how to tell what animal they came from. Now she was nearly as good at it as he.

Here she was, nearly twenty-two, and still unmarried. Likely to remain so if the current status of eligible bachelors in Matson didn't change. Not that she wanted a husband. All the men she knew seemed intent upon pushing her farther away from her fascination with long-dead things. And that she could not tolerate.

She made her way through the crowded exhibition room and out the front door, locking it securely behind her. The museum stood by the wall of the gorge, in the shadow of the undercut layer that hung over the back portion of the building. The Hutchins General Store sat next to the museum, and Elizabeth glanced up and smiled at Lydia Hutchins as she went past.

The Ingram cabin stood at the very outskirts of the town, but she paused in the middle of the packed-earth road. A stagecoach had just pulled up, and a couple of horses she did not recognize were tied to the front of the only hotel in town.

She frowned at the animals as she went by. Standing next to the door was a prospector's backpack, complete with a rock hammer that looked new. Just then the hotel doors opened and a young man stormed out. He stood for a moment, hat in one hand, running the other through his sandy brown hair. His gaze caught hers and he started toward her,

"Here, young lady, wait a moment…"

Wide-eyed, she paused, but her chin raised at the same time. He crossed the street in a few long strides and stopped in front of her. Deep brown eyes stared out from a tanned face, and she was suddenly aware of the dusty smears across the front of her dress.

"Do you happen to know of anywhere a man can get a bath and a bed? The stagecoach beat me into town by a few minutes and there are no more rooms."

Her eyes widened even further, but she said evenly, "Mrs. Goode takes in boarders. I don't know if she has any room just now."

"Can you point me in her direction?"

Elizabeth sighed. Mrs. Goode lived on the far side of the town, across from their cabin, which meant backtracking and she needed to get to the store.

"Meet me here in a few minutes and I'll take you there. I need to stop at the store first."

He beamed, showing a full set of even, white teeth. Nodding, he spun about and made his way back to the hotel steps. She quickened her step on the covered wooden walk to the large storefront with its two paned windows.

"Lizzie!" came a squeal from across the crowded store.

She looked up to see a plump, dark-haired girl moving toward her, parting the way with her hands. "Lizzie, I saw you talking to that young man. Who is he?"

"I don't know…"

"Well, where is he from?"

"I don't know that either…"

"Well then, what is he doing in Matson?"

"Ummm...Lydia, I need to hurry and get some flour and a side of bacon. He is waiting for me to take him to Mrs. Goode's. I'll ask him all your questions."

Lydia Hutchins pushed through the shoppers, mostly women with children clinging to their skirts or begging for one of the candies sitting in the clear jars. She lifted a ten pound sack of flour and called out the door behind the counter for the side of bacon. Within minutes, a boy of about ten came through with something wrapped in newspaper, and Lydia handed them over.

"You might want to remind your pa to come pay the tab. It's been a while..."

Balancing the flour and the wrapped bacon, Elizabeth nodded and left, She hurried along the sidewalk, her boots knocking against the wooden planks. She frowned at the noise; her granny would have had something to say about this unladylike display!

The young man stood, holding his pack. His face cleared as he caught sight of her and he fell into step beside her, after swinging the pack onto his back. They walked for several minutes in silence before he said, "I just realized I don't know your name."

"Elizabeth Ingram. And you?"

"Daniel Bridger. My ma would tan me alive for my manners."

"I was thinking a similar thought about my granny."

He chuckled, his gaze sliding over to look her over. "Am I taking you out of your way?"

She shook her head. "No, I live just there at the end of the street. Mrs. Goode is the next cabin down across the way." She pointed to the spiral of smoke coming from the distant log structure with the large front porch.

He paused and looked down at her. "I thank you, Miss Ingram. I hope we meet again, soon."

She smiled. "Well, if Mrs. Goode can't feed you tonight, you are welcome to join us for supper."

He grinned, showing his remarkable teeth once more. "I may just take you up on that, Miss Ingram." He walked away, leaving her to watch him for a moment before heading into the cabin.

It was empty, of course. Her mother would be out doing her charitable work, and her father would be out at the dig site with the crew. Both would continue until sundown, taking advantage of the light for as long as they could, which would give her time to cook something before her father came home.

It took her a few minutes to start a fire. Then she had to pull out some potatoes from the basket and scrub them outside beside the rain barrel. The carrots were a little rubbery, but she cut them up anyway and threw them into the pot with the potatoes and the last of the roast from Sunday, chopped into bite-size pieces. A large bay leaf went in, with a spoonful of bacon grease for flavor, and she set the food to simmering over the fire. She poured out some of the starter yeast mixture and mixed some more flour and water in before making the sourdough and putting it into the Dutch oven. She shoveled out some embers and set the oven over them, then piled more onto the lid.

Quickly she checked to see if they still had butter, and found a half-paddle full under the ceramic lid of the butter crock. Breathing a sigh of relief, Elizabeth went out the back door and pulled in the laundry from the line. By the time she had finished folding and putting it away, the sun was setting, and she knew it would be about half an hour before her father was home.

The sound of steps on the front porch indicated the arrival of her mother. The door opened and a tall, buxom woman with dark hair gone gray on the sides walked inside. Mrs. Ingram divested herself of her shawl and said, "Goodness, it's cold in here. I had the fire going but it must have died."

"They need to be tended, Ma."

"Yes, well, Mrs. Hutchins told me that the Warshadts' little girl was sick and that Doc Hammond couldn't get there because Mrs. Eldon is having her baby. So I went, and the poor thing was feverish and peaky. Did what I could, likely I'll go back after supper to check on her and see if Doc has made it there yet." She went to the pot and gave the contents a stir.

Elizabeth grabbed the broom and swept the accumulation of sand and dirt from the smooth floorboards. After opening the front door, she brushed the small pile out onto the narrow porch, only to find someone sitting in one of the chairs there.

Silent Jim Smith was a prospector friend of her father's who frequently came by for a meal when the mine didn't provide. He sat now, his beard neatly oiled and brushed, and his balding head well covered by the crown of his hat.

"Mr. Smith, hello! Are you joining us for supper?"

He nodded, cleared his throat, and said quietly, "If I may."

"Of course. Father will be back soon. Can I get you some water?"

He shook his head and went back to contemplating

the dirt beyond the porch. She swished inside to stir the stew and add a little flour to thicken the broth, then counted the tin plates to make sure there was enough in case Mr. Bridger came as well. As long as no other unexpected visitors arrived, there would be enough.

A hearty "halloo" came from the front of the cabin and she heard a single response come from Silent Jim. Her father stood and talked for some minutes about the specimen he and the crew of two others were digging free of the Colorado formation.

"A sauropod, probably *Brontosaurus*, or the new *Camarasaurus* that Cope described last year. We have the whole back end, and some Oligocene fossils from the lower creek site. Lizzie's working on those at the museum."

She opened the door and looked out to see her father standing next to the implements and rucksack he had set down on the porch. Silent Jim nodded and smiled, listening to her father's effusion as though he understood it all, and perhaps he did. It was difficult to know just what Jim Smith understood beneath the quiet exterior. She glanced up toward Mrs. Goode's but saw no movement from that direction. The gorge dissolved into the shadow of twilight and she set a candle in the only glass window of the cabin, in case Mr. Bridger came later.

"Supper is ready, Father, Mr. Smith. Ma."

"Ah! Lizzie! We reached a scapula today, it gives me great hope that a skull is waiting!" He ladled up some stew and spoke between mouthfuls.

Silent Jim followed suit, but did not speak, simply shoveled food in and seemed to savor it.

"That would mean an entire specimen! Are there

any others?"

"It is too early to tell and I have not personally examined Cope's specimen. We must wait for the analysis this winter. But what a find! I look forward to writing this up. She has become a good luck charm!"

"She?"

"There is something rather gracile about the femur which led me to ponder whether or not it might be female."

"She, then. I may accompany you to the field tomorrow."

Just then, a knock came at the door. Elizabeth set her bowl down and went to unlatch it. There stood Daniel, looking somewhat cleaner and dressed in fresh clothes.

He smiled and said, "I was hoping the invitation still stood. Mrs. Goode suggested I would be better fed here as she had not planned on boarders tonight."

Elizabeth's mouth crooked upward, and she moved back to allow him in. He stepped past her and she shut the door, before picking up the last of the plates and ladling up a healthy amount of the stew.

"Pa, Ma, Mr. Smith, this is Daniel Bridger. He's new to Matson. Mr. Bridger, this is my father, Wilberforce Ingram..."

"Bones," Silent Jim said.

She chuckled. "Yes, we call him Bones. Or Dr. Ingram. And this is my mother, Elsebeth Ingram."

"Very nice to meet you, Mr. Bridger. Do make yourself at home."

"Thank you."

Her father and Silent Jim both nodded to him, then Dr. Ingram went back to the paper he was reading.

Daniel went to sit, but then stopped.

"Where will you sit? This is the last seat."

Silent Jim stood abruptly and handed Elizabeth his empty plate. "I'm off. Thank ye." He nodded around to everyone before opening and shutting the door quietly behind him.

Elizabeth placed his empty plate and spoon into the basin and sat, then picked up her bowl once more. For a few minutes there was only the sound of eating, then Dr. Ingram looked up and closed the book.

"I apologize, very rude of me, and bad for the eyes reading with so little light."

"Not at all, continue if you are so inclined," Daniel said.

"Bones can socialize. Can't you?" Ma said.

"Yes, Elsie. I can." He turned to Daniel and added, "Where are you from?"

"I'm from Philadelphia. Heard about the frontier and wanted to see it for myself." He looked down as he said this, then his intense brown gaze caught Elizabeth's and he smiled. "What do you do in Matson?"

"I am a fossil prospector. Just now I am…er, you are not affiliated with Cope or Marsh, are you?"

Daniel shook his head, "I assure you that although I am familiar with their names, I have no affinity for either."

"Well, that is good. If you have heard of them, you are no doubt aware of the ruinous feud going on between them. It has been my endeavor to avoid both in my work, but yet they will find out about my discoveries and pressure me to turn over my finds."

"That must be frustrating. How do you keep your

work from them?"

"Well, we are a small operation. Only me and a few helpers, miners whose mines gave out. They work for very little pay and an occasional meal."

"How kind of you."

"I don't know how kind it is. I feel that they might be better off going home, but they want to stay and I need the help, so…"

He nodded thoughtfully, then turned to Elizabeth. "And you, Miss Elizabeth? What do you do here?"

"I work in Pa's museum and help keep house. Ma is often busy doing work in the community. She was a nurse when younger, and is a marvelous asset to Matson. I just help out where I can."

"She is being ingenuous. Elizabeth is one of the best fossil preparers I have ever known. Just now she is working on an oreodont skull that we found a few weeks ago in a separate site. Well, obviously. Oreodonts are mammals and therefore the skull is much younger than the dinosaur we are working on."

"Of course, that makes perfect sense. Which species of oreodont is it?"

"We are not sure. We need to see comparable specimens at the Peabody and Smithsonian. But funds are scarce so I shall simply have to order the publications that show the unique features among the family."

"I have been to both. They have remarkable collections."

Elizabeth was caught by the sudden realization that it was a small admission, and that they still knew very little about Daniel Bridger. And yet, he was learning quite a bit about them.

"Did you want another helping?" she asked.

He leaned back and smiled at her. "I should say no, but that was excellent. I will take some more, thank you." He motioned for her to sit and stood to dish it up himself. She sat slowly, eyes wide at the gallant gesture. Then she remembered how little they knew of him and asked,

"Do your parents approve of your travels?"

He glanced down, then his gaze found hers once again. "Oh, well, they have no reason not to approve."

"Where do they live?"

"Back home. Philadelphia."

His answers came easily...too easily? For some reason she felt that he was hiding something. But his expression seemed open as he gazed evenly back at her. The corner of his mouth crooked upward as though reading her mind and challenging her.

Her chin lifted a little and she asked, "Are you planning to mine, or homestead?"

"Just keeping my options open."

"Yes, but there aren't that many options in Matson."

"Lizzie, don't quiz the man so. He's our guest," Ma said.

"Just asking, Ma."

"Well, I may press on toward Denver, or head for the Morrison dig. Still unsettled in my plans. Always been fascinated by fossils and such; maybe I'll stay on and work with your father if he'll have me."

Dr. Ingram lifted an eyebrow. "As long as you aren't expecting any pay."

Daniel laughed and rose to set his plate in the basin. "No, sir. I would consider it a privilege. I will think on what you have said. But I have kept you both up rather late. I'll say goodnight." He smiled at them all and strode to the door before disappearing into the night.

Elizabeth watched him go with a quickening heartbeat. She found she was quite interested in Daniel Bridger.

Chapter Two

Daniel let loose a long sigh as he walked through the dark toward Mrs. Goode's home. Things had become suddenly very complicated for him. He thought back to the first time he had seen Elizabeth Ingram. She had been looking down, then lifted her head and stared straight at him with her hazel eyes. He'd been caught unawares, and that was no good for a man in his position.

He kicked the dust off his heels and climbed the steps onto the porch of the boarding house. Though rustic compared to his home back in Philadelphia, it was reasonably clean. Mrs. Goode seemed rather too interested in his background, but he would be able to put her off. Indeed, he had to. No one must know who he really was.

For starters, though Daniel was his name, Bridger was nothing more than the maiden name of his favorite aunt back home. The Company had insisted he change his name, and he had not argued the point. Not even his parents knew what he was up to.

He paused climbing the steps to his room. He owed them at least a note telling them he had reached his destination. What to say? That he was a spy in the camp and he had made first contact? No.

He would tell them he had reached Denver. That, at least, was not a lie even if it were not the whole truth.

Matson lay in a large cut in the foothills of the Great Rocky Mountains, just southwest of Denver. He had traveled by train to Denver, then purchased his pack and implements and his supplies. Finding the coach had left, he had hitched a ride on a passing hay wagon to get to Matson. He had his instructions, and he had followed them.

He closed the door behind him. Someone—he presumed Mrs. Goode—had lit the lantern for him and the room glowed in the soft light. Shadows moved and shook as he sat on the bed and pulled his boots off. The room was chilly, and he hastened under the covers once he had stripped down and pulled on a nightshirt. He stared at the lantern's circular glow on the ceiling for a moment before turning it down to almost nothing. The light flickered and slowly died, and the shadows spread to cover everything. A thin shaft of silver moonlight straggled in through the curtains.

His mind circled around, eyes focused on the thin light casting patterns through the curtains. What to do about this latest development? He had been struck down by a single glance. That girl had the potential to become a distraction, and here he had a job to do. Somehow he would need to keep his head—no daughter of bones was going to interfere in his duty!

****

Morning came and with it, new-found purpose. Today he would infiltrate the dig if at all possible. He thought that Dr. Ingram would welcome his help on the site, and that would give him a chance to get information from the other men. It would serve the added benefit of keeping him clear of the fair Elizabeth. He did not trust himself around her…

Mrs. Goode provided a simple breakfast of gruel, thick and gummy. It clung to the spoon and to the sides of the bowl, making eating it trickier than he had time for. He managed to clear half the bowl before ceding defeat and setting down his spoon. Before he could change his mind, Mrs. Goode had snatched it up and carried it off, presumably to the kitchen.

He stretched, then tightened one suspender before pulling on his coat and heading out. The early morning air was cold, and Mrs. Goode had been stingy with the wood in the fireplace. He rubbed his hands together and blew out a long breath, then smiled and headed for the museum.

The door was open and he stepped inside, trying not to squeak the floorboards too loudly. Sounds of sweeping came to him, and suddenly she was there, wrangling a broom and attacking the floor with carefully modulated strokes. She glanced his way and her face lit up in a way that stopped his heart for a moment.

"Mr. Bridger! You have just missed my father."

"Where has he gone?"

"He went down to the tavern to solicit some help for the dig. Sometimes he can find miners who are down on their luck and don't mind wielding a pick axe for a few pennies."

"Well, that is what I am here for. I have come to join the dig."

Hazel eyes looked into his. "Are you sure? Only, I thought you were bound for the Morrison site."

"A man can change his mind, can't he?"

She laughed—a marvelous sound—and bent to sweep under a table. "Yes, why not. We shall be happy to have you. As long as you don't want too much in the way of financial recompense."

He felt himself grin. He liked this girl. "I am more interested in the experience than anything."

"Well, that we can give you." She brushed the dust and debris out the front door and into the street before coming in and disappearing into the back room, then reappearing with an apron and sans broom. She pinned the bib of the apron to her bodice and tied its strings about her waist. "You might as well wait here—Father will be back momentarily. He left his hat, and will not venture far without it."

She sat at the table and picked up the little pick, then began gently scraping at the rock surrounding the skull on the sand-filled tray on the table. He leaned close, and noticed her hair was a simple braid coiled about the back of her head. It smelled faintly of roses and he breathed it in, lost for a moment. Forcing himself to pay attention, he noted that she was left-handed and that she did nothing to hide it. As she worked, the rock matrix gave way, falling aside with each scrape of the thin blade to reveal the lighter bone within.

"That's a fine skull."

"We have the entire skeleton, but I couldn't wait and had to start on the skull even though it is barely spring."

"Do you usually prep and study in the winter then?"

She nodded. "We are usually too busy digging in the spring and summer, sometimes into the fall. Father will push the season times... We were shut down by a blizzard last year before he gave in."

Laughter bubbled out of him. "An ideal paleontologist, then."

"Well, I think so. He has published his fair share of papers, though Cope and Marsh of course overshadow him. Both have tried to get hold of our specimens."

His attention quickened. "Both of them?"

She nodded again, scraping the sandstone from the orbit of the skull. "They have both sent their spies to work on us. Father has eluded them. All of our specimens come here, and then some are sold to collectors, and some are shipped out to a museum back east that pays handsomely for them."

"Which one?"

"The Continental Museum of Natural History in Connecticut."

His eyes widened, "I have been there! It is a fine establishment."

She lifted her face to his, and he realized how close he was to her. She caught her breath, and her eyes flicked to his mouth and then back up.

"Yes, it is. At least, so I've heard. I have not been myself."

"Where did you grow up." He pulled away slightly, reluctantly.

"Here. I was born in Connecticut, but father and mother came out here shortly after I was born. This is the only life I know."

A voice called from the doorway just then. "Elizabeth, meet Morty Swanson! I found him at the tavern and he has agreed to join us."

She looked over to her father and the grizzled, pugnacious-looking man beside him. He doffed his hat in her direction and his squinty gaze traveled around the room.

Daniel pulled away from her and said, "Sir, I was hoping you'd allow me to join you as well."

Ingram grinned his gap-toothed smile. "We would be most happy to have you. It is a good hour's trek into the hills to get to the site."

"Then you had best get started." Elizabeth shot a glance at the clock and then back down to the skull.

Her father squinted and then waved him along toward the door. "True. Let's get going, boys. I hope you don't mind hard work. You have your own bedroll?"

"I'll come back to stay at Mrs. Goode's each evening."

"Fine, fine. Let's get moving."

Daniel glanced back toward Elizabeth. Her face was turned down toward the fossil before her, but her eyes flashed up at him and he gave her a smile. Then he followed her father out into the sunshine.

He breathed deeply, letting the dry air fill his lungs. The sunrise had lit the mountains up with yellows and reds and newly-emerged greens. He had to fight to keep himself from feeling enamored with it all. The last thing he wanted was to become attached to this place with its wide spaces and brilliant colors. And an intelligent, beautiful girl thrown in…

Ingram led them down a path through the scrub and red hills. They ascended the rise in a twisted path, then down into a ravine. Pine trees dotted the hillsides, providing intermittent shade from the increasing heat of the sun. The cloudless sky spread blue overhead, and excitement surged in Daniel.

After an hour they rounded a rise and dropped into

a little valley overhung with a slab of sandstone. Three scruffy men labored on a spread of rock there. One large man wielded a pickaxe while another used a hammer and chisel. The third filled a wooden bucket with rocks and sand to carry off and dump on a growing pile some yards away.

Ingram went immediately to where the big man with the pickaxe stood, wiping his brow. "Well, Henry, how goes it?"

The man nodded down toward the ground and Ingram knelt to examine the rock. Daniel's head tilted to one side as he watched. The paleontologist's hands moved over the rock and his focus intensified.

"This is a series of neck vertebra we've found. With luck we'll hit a skull at the end of it." He turned and looked at the men. "We'll be focusing on this area for now. I need to know how complete a specimen we have."

Morty reached for a spare pickaxe and moved toward the top of the overburden. Daniel stepped up to look. He could see the slightly paler bone embedded in the rock. He reached into his pack to retrieve the chisel and hammer he had purchased the day before. With a look at Ingram, he knelt down, placed the chisel and hit it with the hammer, angling it to chip the rock from the bone. Work continued on around him as he focused on the bone beneath his fingers, and chiseling it free from the rock around it.

Now and then he paused, closed his eyes and felt the rock beneath his hands. There would be a rough sensation like sandpaper, then smoothness of bone. He found also that if he dripped some water from his canteen on the rock, it would darken, whereas the bone would not.

The sun beat down, burning his exposed neck and the skin beneath the part in his hair. Sweat dampened his shirt and he remembered to drink often from his canteen. When the sun was directly overhead, Ingram called them to a halt and they gathered around the fire for warm cider and stale bread with a hefty piece of jerky. The gruel from Mrs. Goode had not lasted long, and Daniel was relieved to get some food into his gut.

The day passed, and by the end of it, he had chiseled nearly an entire side of a vertebra out. He slipped his tools into his pack and followed Ingram down the path once again. The rest of the men apparently camped at the site. He noted they pulled out more jerky and bread from a pack suspended from a tall tripod off the ground. Personally, he hoped for better at Elizabeth's table... if Ingram would invite him.

"That was good work of yours. I am glad to see you so skilled with the chisel. Where did you work before?"

"Oh, I volunteered with local crews out east whenever possible."

"At this rate, we will hopefully reach the skull before the end of the month. I begin to suspect it is *Camarasaurus* as described by Cope last year. The neck vertebrae are chambered, as he indicated, and so I strongly hypothesize that is what we have."

"It would be an exciting find."

He sighed. "Not so exciting as a new species."

"True. Perhaps this is a new species of *Camarasaurus*?"

"It is possible, depending upon the age of the fossil. We will know more as we dig."

"Are the men staying at the site?"

"Yes. They are all armed."

"Is that necessary?"

"Unfortunately, yes. Not only are Cope and Marsh pressing for dinosaur finds, but a local man, Stanthorpe Wilke, is also known to steal sites. If we leave the bones unguarded, we might come back to find another team had claimed them."

In the distance, down the slope, the lights of the Ingram cabin glowed. Across the way, the Goode house rose. Daniel bit his lip. Ingram had still not invited him to supper, and he wondered how he might turn the conversation.

"Ah, I wonder what Elizabeth has fashioned for supper tonight!" Ingram said.

"It will be delicious, no matter what, I am sure. Hopefully Mrs. Goode's fare is its equal."

"Ha! Mrs. Goode is no cook. There will be food, yes, but not much to tempt the palate. Join us, there is always plenty."

"I would feel bad if Mrs. Goode prepared something for me…"

"If she did, you will most certainly have it for breakfast, so don't worry. Here we are, Elsie, Elizabeth! We are home!"

Elizabeth turned from the stove, a tendril of hair framing one half of her face. "Father, and Mr. Bridger! Supper is just about ready. Go get cleaned up and we'll sit down."

"Where is your mother?" Ingram asked.

"She is back at the Warshadts' looking after their little girl. The child did not pass a good night and Ma is worried." She motioned them out the door.

"Out to the rain barrel for us!"

A bowl of soap sat on a small table beside the rain barrel. They sluiced the water down their arms and splashed their faces before scooping up a small amount of soap and working it into a lather. Then they scrubbed their arms and faces clean, rinsing off with clean water afterward. A small towel lay on the table, and they dried off with it.

A fresh loaf of sourdough bread filled the cabin with a wonderful smell. Elizabeth ladled up a thick soup into the ceramic bowls. All of them were chipped, and had different patterns adorning their sides. Daniel watched where the others sat and then took the unoccupied space. Ingram reached for a thick slice of bread and quickly spread some of the butter on it. Daniel did the same and took a bite of the warm bread with melting butter. Then he dipped his spoon into the stew-like soup and tasted it.

"This is really excellent!"

Elizabeth colored, but smiled. "Thank you."

"You are very welcome. Is this what you did all day?"

She laughed, an easy sound. "No, indeed. I spent the morning working in the museum. In the afternoon I did laundry, then hung it out to dry while I got supper going. Today I classified some of the new finds that have been prepared. We are getting quite the mammal selection."

"Mammals are often overlooked in these dinosaur-mad times," he said.

She smiled. "You're so right. And yet I find them interesting, from a selfish point of view perhaps seeing as how we are mammals as well. It's like taking a glimpse into our past."

He looked into her hazel eyes, now staring so earnestly at him and his heart jumped. It was difficult to remember he had a job to perform, and that such feelings as she was engendering had no place in it. He looked down and attacked his meal for a few minutes to try and distance himself, but it was difficult.

Ingram leaned back and sighed. "I must pay our tab at the general store. We will be needing more supplies to keep the crew fed and meat is expensive."

"I was thinking of getting a few chickens for the eggs. Mrs. Heggedy has a clutch of eggs right now."

Ingram's head tilted to one side as he did some mental sums. "How much will she want for them?"

"A nickel each. But think of the eggs we would get!"

"Yes, yes. All right, lay claim to them. But we will need a hutch for them to roost in at night to keep them safe from dogs and foxes. And coyotes."

"I can help build one. I have built several in my time." Elizabeth looked up and her jaw dropped. "That would be wonderful. Thank you, Mr. Bridger. Though I don't want to impose on your work with Father."

"I can spare him for a day or two. He is a remarkably gifted worker, however. He does nearly the work of two men out there!"

His cheeks grew hot, and he swallowed his embarrassment. "It's nothing. I like the work."

He looked up to see Elizabeth beaming at him.

"How long are you staying in Matson?"

His mouth dropped open, and he thought fast. "A while, anyway. Perhaps for the season. I don't know…" He faltered beneath her gaze.

Her smile faded and she looked down. "Well, we will be happy to have you as long as you will stay."

Just then the door opened and Mrs. Ingram bustled in. She laid a shawl on a wooden bench and sighed. "Poor little mite. She isn't doing as well as I'd like. The fever is peaking. We got her comfortable and I said I'd come home for a short while to eat and then be back. I didn't want to burden them by eating there." She sat at the table, dished up a plateful, and ate quickly.

They finished their meal in silence, then he offered to help clean up, but Elizabeth refused.

"Father will enjoy having someone besides me to talk to."

Mrs. Ingram set her plate down, kissed the balding head of her husband, and bustled back out. Bones Ingram stood and went to the fire, gesturing for Daniel to join him.

The wooden chair beside the fireplace welcomed him as he sat. Ingram had pulled out a pipe and was puffing gently on it.

"Do you mind it?" he asked.

"Not at all, sir." He inhaled a bit of the smoke and coughed discreetly. Ingram read from a journal and Daniel surreptitiously watched Elizabeth as she darted about, cleaning up after the meal and tidying the cabin before coming to sit as well beside the fire. She leaned back and closed her eyes for a moment before reaching for the basket at her feet and pulling out a half-finished sock on the needles.

"Is your work never done?" he asked.

She shook her head. "Never. Though my work in the museum is mostly relaxing, I will admit. Working on the bones and preparing them is more fun than work, and I enjoy it immensely."

"That is ideal then…" His voice faded away as they shared a glance. He forced himself to break it almost instantly and cursed his tender feelings.

How was he going to handle them and yet keep his mind clear for the job ahead?

Chapter Three

The room swirled a bit as she stared into Daniel's eyes. They were dark brown, and seemed depthless in the firelight. To hide her confusion, for a while she focused on the sock she was knitting until she heard him stand.

"I must get back to Mrs. Goode's. Thank you for a wonderful evening."

"Of course," she heard herself say. "You are always welcome."

He avoided her eyes and she frowned a little at this. He left without a backward look and this hurt somehow. She gave herself a shake and peered through the firelight at the stocking hanging from her needles. Her father was quiet as he read his *Western Naturalist* journal. Sighing, she set the sock down in the basket and rose.

"Good night, Father."

"Oh!" he said, lifting his head. "Is it that time already?"

"For me, yes." She kissed him on the top of his head before heading up the stairs.

The loft was cold. She set the candle down on her dressing table and pulled out the hair pins so she could take down her hair and brush it out. She shivered as she undressed in the thin light. Once the corset was off, she stretched from side to side and breathed deeply before climbing in between the icy sheets.

"Brrr."

She shuddered as warmth began finally to build under the covers. But it wasn't the skull waiting for her at the museum or the last bit of ham hanging from the rafters to be used for the morrow's supper that filled her mind.

Rather, it was the deep brown gaze of her father's newest protégé that captured her thoughts.

****

Morning light straggled through the high clouds into the main room of the museum. Her father and Daniel had already left, Daniel with hardly a glance in her direction. She stared at her reflection in the small mirror she carried in her large pocket. Lightly tanned features, no surprise given her propensity to venture outside. Tiny freckles dusted her nose. Her lips were a fine rose color, and something she was ashamedly proud of. Hazel eyes and eyebrows seemingly perpetually raised in query completed her look. Certainly not elegantly beautiful like Charlotte Janney, she thought, but well-looking enough.

Fair enough for Daniel Bridger?

With a sigh, she angled the mirror to catch the light and direct it down onto the skull to help her differentiate the bone there. Then she began work on it just as the door opened and a gust of wind swirled through the room. She looked up to see a handsome man in fine clothes appear. Sunlight shone from behind him, lighting up his golden hair like a halo. She caught her breath.

"I am looking for the museum of Dr. Ingram. Have I found it?"

She stood. "Yes, I am Elizabeth Ingram."

He came forward, his shining boots sounding against the wooden planks of the floor. He gave a small bow and then straightened to look directly at her. One side of his mouth crept up and he said,

"I am delighted to make your acquaintance. I am Rufus Howell, of the Richmond Howells. I am here on behalf of Stanthorpe Wilke, You may have heard of him?"

"I think there are few people on the Front Range who have not! The Denver millionaire who collects fossils."

"Yes. I have a crew and a claim he has staked to dig."

"Where is it?"

"Ah…that I am not at liberty to say. It is a secret."

"Mmm, I see. What age is the stratum you are working—Jurassic or Cretaceous?"

His mouth dropped open. "I have said too much already. I am here to request your father join us in our work."

"But, he has his own site to dig; he is a busy man."

"Wilke would make it well worth his while."

His critical gaze traveled over the ramshackle tables and the clutter of casts and rocks waiting to be prepped. Elizabeth felt he must also know about the pressing tab at the general store by the look on his face. Luckily the mend in her apron was hidden by the table.

"I will ask him when he comes home this evening, but I think I can tell you what his answer will be."

"And what is that?"

"Something along the lines of 'go to the devil!'"

Rufus tipped his head back and laughed. "He may

regret that attitude. There are consequences to stubbornness and pride."

Her eyebrows met and her chin lifted. "Are you threatening us?"

He smiled. "No, no, of course not. Simply stating a fact. Please give him my message. I'm staying at the High Hotel across from the Town Hall before I head out to the site in a day or two."

Still aglow in the sunlight, he backed out of the door and disappeared. Elizabeth stared at the closed door where he had been just moments before. Breathing deeply, she tried to focus on the oreodont skull, but found she couldn't. Her thoughts had scattered. She pushed up from the table and went to the front window, where she stood looking out.

The town had wakened and now people were beginning to crowd the wooden sidewalk. She wondered how the dig was going. In particular, what Daniel was doing. Suddenly the thought of being indoors all day was impossible to think about and she pulled a canteen free from the equipment table to fill up at the creek. After snatching her shawl up, she strapped on her belt with its hammer and chisels, and headed out.

The way to the dig site was well-trodden, and she was not afraid to walk it alone, though she suddenly realized she never had. Always she had been with someone else... Never alone. The path meandered along around rock outcroppings and uplifted sandstone slabs. Ponderosa pine and the occasional aspen tree were scattered about, with plenty of tall grasses and brush to fill the space in between. Perhaps half an hour passed when the hair on the back of her neck stood up.

Casting about, she drew her shawl closer and

quickened her step. But as she rounded a corner, she nearly bumped into the tall form of Edgar Collins. He looked down at her as he steadied her with a hand to the shoulder.

"Miss Ingram," he said, and his accent betrayed his Ute ancestry.

Why he lived apart from his people, no one knew, only that he worked a claim deep in the hills, and came into town occasionally to trade. He spoke little, and moved silently.

"Mr. Collins."

"You should not be here alone. Bad men have come to the mountains."

"Who?"

But he was looking off into the distance and did not seem to hear. Instead, he moved off the path so she could walk by. "Are you going to your father?"

"Yes," she said breathlessly, then swallowed. "The site is not far off."

He leaned close suddenly, and she gasped. "Do not let them take it," he whispered, then he was gone.

Elizabeth stared after him, then fumbled with her canteen to take a drink. Her mind awhirl, she set off again. What had Edgar meant by that? The air felt a little colder to her, and she bunched the shawl around her exposed neck.

Perhaps it was her quickened pace, but soon enough she reached the edge of her father's camp. And when she came around the edge of the uplifted slabs of sandstone, she met face-to-face with Daniel.

His dark eyes widened, and her mouth dropped open.

"Hello, Mr. Bridger."

"Miss Ingram! What are you doing here?"

"I came to lend a hand."

"Alone?"

"As you see."

"But that is a preposterous risk you took."

"What risk? I walked for an hour upon a path in the foothills."

"But…" he spluttered and hot anger shafted through Elizabeth.

"I think I can be trusted to determine where and when I shall walk, Mr. Bridger."

"Elizabeth?" Her father's voice came from underneath the sandstone shelf. "Is that you? Oh, excellent. I have reached one of the distal neck vertebrae and it requires your delicate hand."

She smiled and ducked around Daniel to go to where her father knelt on the ground. She folded her shawl and arranged it on the ground beside the spot her father indicated. After kneeling upon it, she unhooked her hammer and medium-sized chisel from her belt, then brushed the dirt away. The bone was distinct from the sandstone, but only just, and the niche was shaded for the moment. She pulled out her mirror and angled it in the sunlight, directing its beam downward onto the bone. Then she picked up the hammer and chisel.

Sensing eyes upon her, she glanced around to find Daniel nearby, watching her. He looked down abruptly and began to work, leaving her to smile and bend over her own place on the dinosaur's neck. The edges of the vertebra were becoming clearer, and she switched to her larger chisel to chip away at the sandstone as she dug down around the bone.

"Please forgive my overbearing attitude, Miss

Ingram."

"Not at all, Mr. Bridger."

"Do you come out to the dig often, Miss Ingram?"

The hammer strikes on the chisels echoed in the niche, and she had to focus to hear what he said. "I come when I can. I had a visitor at the museum this morning I wish to tell Father about, but he is busy at the moment."

Dr. Ingram could be heard providing instructions to the newest members of the crew. "No, angle it away from the bone, never toward. You must protect the bone! Morty, careful with the shovel. Use the broom to sweep up the rocks and sand from the fossils."

"Who came?"

"A Rufus Howell, on behalf of Stanthorpe Wilke. Have you heard of either?"

He was silent for a moment, then his hammer came down with extra force upon the chisel. "Yes, I know of them. They are trouble."

"That is what I thought. Rufus practically threatened Father." She repeated the conversation and Daniel's mouth became grim.

"That was a threat all right. He means to take over this dig site."

"That's what Edgar hinted at. What can we do?"

"I don't know. Your father may have an idea…"

Just then Dr. Ingram turned toward them, "Elizabeth, how goes that vertebra?"

"Good, Father." She then recounted what she had told Daniel about Rufus and Edgar. Her father's bushy eyebrows came together and he seemed to consider.

"Stanthorpe Wilke, eh?"

"Yes. He's powerful…"

"Yes, but he can't actually take my claim over. It is mine, to yield or not. I will not yield, so we must simply ignore their attempts."

"But, Father—"

"No, Elizabeth. I say it will be well. We must simply hold firm and eventually they will honor that."

"Edgar seems to think there are bad men in the hills…perhaps he means them. If so, they may not work with honor."

"I cannot see a paleontologist stealing another's claim."

"But Cope and Marsh—" Daniel began.

"Yes, yes, Cope and Marsh. But their enmity surpasses paleontology. We need not emulate them or expect everyone to take on as they do."

Daniel turned a worried expression to Elizabeth. She sat back and traced the edge of the bone with her finger.

"I fear we are in for a rough time, whether he believes it or not," she said softly and he nodded.

"I think you are right. I may start sleeping out here to help guard the site."

"But Mrs. Goode…?"

"I will save a bit on room and board."

She smiled shortly. "That is true."

The sun had found the niche by now and was beating down on them. Sweat had begun to bead along her forehead and her neck was warm. She sprinkled some water from her canteen onto the folded edge of her shawl and wrapped it loosely around her neck.

"I see a shawl serves many purposes."

She grinned at him. "Indeed, they do. I would never go anywhere without one."

"I'm at a disadvantage."

"A neckerchief can come in nearly as handy."

"I must make sure to get one next time I am at the store."

They worked for a while in companionable silence, with nothing but the clinks of hammer upon chisel to break it. There was the occasional expletive when the hammer slipped from the chisel and hit a hand instead. By the time they paused for lunch, both sported reddened knuckles.

"I'm quite rusty at this," Elizabeth said.

Her father clapped her on the shoulder. "You spend too much time indoors, working in the museum and around the cabin. I need another three of you to be happy."

She laughed. "I think one of me is ample."

Her father moved quickly back to his spot near the front of the dinosaur and she returned to her place on its neck. The sun shone orange-red off the sandstone sides of the gully and the sky was a clear medium blue. Her father smiled at her all of a sudden, then went back to work.

All seemed well, but she could not dispel a sense of foreboding.

Chapter Four

Daniel wiped his forehead with his handkerchief, then replaced it in his pocket. He was still unnerved by hearing about Stanthorpe Wilke. The millionaire was known for his dirty deals and desire to gain dinosaur fossils at all costs. He knew him better than he had let on. But surely Wilke wouldn't stoop to the lowest levels...

He rubbed his sore knuckles and risked another glance at Elizabeth. The sun glinted gold off her brown hair and a single lock slipped free and fell into her face. With an impatient noise, she tucked it behind her ear and returned to her work on the fossil. He'd never met a girl like her—was there anything she could not do?

The afternoon grew hot, and he perspired freely, kneeling on the heated ground in the sun. Elizabeth, too, had damp tendrils of hair clinging to her face and neck, and still she worked. There was a streak of dirt on her brow where she had wiped away sweat with a dirty hand. He smiled to himself at it.

As the sun settled behind the mountain, it grew too dark to continue to work and they quickly packed up. The men who were staying at the site clustered around the fire, eating their flatbread and jerky, while Dr. Ingram and his daughter headed back to Matson with him in tow.

Elizabeth walked ahead of him, and he tried to

catch up to her. Her canteen clanked lightly against the hammer in her belt and he could smell the sweat coming from himself. The was a small tear near the hem of Elizabeth's skirt; in his mind he could see her sitting beside the fire in their cabin and mending it.

She motioned to the top of the ridge with her hand and his gaze followed. A figure silhouetted there against the sky. Dr. Ingram lifted a hand to the figure, but it did not move, simply regarded them from on high.

Hunger pains caused him to swallow and he hoped Mrs. Goode had a decent dinner for the evening. He could hear Dr. Ingram talking aloud, presumably to Elizabeth who answered with "Oh, yes," and "Ah," from time to time.

They all clustered around the rain barrel, washing up and Elizabeth disappeared, only to return with three more cloths to dry their arms and faces. She sighed.

"I've made nothing for supper, and Ma is not home."

"Hmmm. Perhaps we should go to the hotel for supper."

Daniel cleared his throat. "I suppose I had better get to Mrs. Goode's."

"Nonsense, come with us. They have reasonable rates for their suppers." He looked at Elizabeth, "We shall have to get a plate for your mother."

He glanced at Elizabeth, whose expression betrayed nothing. "Well, if you insist. Are we quite dressed well enough?"

"I should think so. This isn't Denver after all."

"Then I would be happy to join you."

He angled himself to walk beside Elizabeth as they

headed toward the tallest building in town. The High Hotel had been built by Reginald Janney just before the gold rush and he had made his fortune on it. Now the mayor of Matson, he courted dignitaries from all over to come to his hotel in the foothills of the Rocky Mountains.

Elizabeth smoothed her hair back and twitched her skirt a little. He smiled at these tell-tale signs of nervousness. And though her dress was faded, the pale green brought out her hazel eyes and made them shine. Her cheeks glowed like peaches from the day in the sun and he could barely look at her lips without wanting to taste them.

He glanced around as they entered and was surprised. The hotel was luxurious. Velvet curtains and gold trim were everywhere. The floor was polished smooth and shone like marble, leaving him to wonder if that was what it was. The host's glance looked them over, then motioned for them to follow him.

They were seated at a nondescript corner of the bar where no one would be likely to see them and given a quick rundown of the supper for the evening. It was venison and quail, with a vegetable he could not hear due to the background noise of the bar. The plates were brought out and the three of them tucked in. Warm yeast bread was placed on their table with fresh cream butter. It was a surprising meal for the little town.

A ruckus near the staircase drew his attention and he strained to look at what was going on. Two well-dressed men in suits and fine vests stood at the base of the grand staircase. A large man, like a cadaverous shadow, hung in the background.

Elizabeth leaned toward him, pointed to the

rounder of the three men and said, "That's Reginald Janney, with his man Will Gunn, but I don't know who he is with."

He leaned closer. "I do. That's Stanthorpe Wilke. What is he doing here in Matson?"

But Dr. Ingram was standing, patting his stomach and motioning them to follow him. As they passed by Stanthorpe, he paused in what he was saying and peered at Elizabeth, then up to her father.

With his gaze still on her, he said, "Dr. Ingram? Yes, I recognize you from your photo in *Western Naturalist.*"

"Yes sir, to whom am I speaking?"

"This is Stanthorpe Wilke, Ingram. From Denver," Mayor Janney said.

"Oh, yes of course. Good evening, sir."

"Back from a long day at the site?" Stanthorpe asked.

"Yes, very busy day. Nearly got another vertebra out and the scapula is coming free with the humerus and a few ribs. That will be a large cast to transport."

"I would be happy to take over the site for you." Wilke's steely blue gaze burned toward Ingram.

"Nonsense, nonsense. I have it all in hand. Well, thank you Janney, excellent supper. Good night!"

He headed off and Daniel followed, but not before the blue gaze was turned upon him. He could feel it setting the back of his head on fire and tried not to hurry away. They reached the point where he needed to head across the road and down a bit to Mrs. Goode's and he hesitated. Though he'd had little enough to say to her, he still wanted to linger beside Elizabeth.

She turned to him and smiled. "Good night, Mr.

Bridger."

"Good night, Miss Ingram. Dr. Ingram."

"See you bright and early. We're going to push to reach the skull tomorrow!"

"That will be exciting." He watched them go, and then smiled to see Elizabeth glance back toward him.

Mrs. Goode's felt cold and empty after the camaraderie of the evening. He sought her out in her little office. Her round face looked up, sour expression unchanged.

"Yes? No complaints." She made it a statement.

"No, ma'am. But I will be staying at the dig site, starting tomorrow."

"Sounds uncomfortable."

"Certainly not so comfortable as here, but necessary."

"Well then, might as well square up." She named a price for the nights he had stayed and he quickly paid.

The upstairs room was cold, but he washed up anyways and changed into his nightshirt. He'd be sleeping in his clothes from here on out, and hated to think what he would end up smelling like. He lay down on the lumpy mattress and ignored the rustling of the straw ticking and the squeak of the ropes beneath it. Sleep seemed far away. And yet it caught him quickly and held him captive until dawn.

He woke with a start, disoriented by his dreams of being trapped underground and running out of air. He dressed quickly, placed his belongings in his pack and hoisted it up to carry downstairs. A family had come in the night and were seated around the table. A mother who looked like a Madonna, a father with a lantern jaw, and a boy of about eight who frowned at Daniel.

Mrs. Goode had prepared more gruel—watery this time. He forced himself to eat an entire bowlful under the unblinking stare of the boy.

"Are you a dinosaur hunter?"

Daniel's mouth dropped open, and he closed it rapidly. "I suppose I am. Do you like dinosaurs?"

"I should say so! My favorites are the carnivores. Father bought me a tooth; it is four inches long!"

"That's quite a tooth."

"I'm going to be a dinosaur hunter when I grow up. I'm going to carry a pistol and shoot anyone who dares try to steal my fossils."

"Now, Theo, don't talk so. You would never shoot someone," his mother said.

"If they tried to take my bones I would."

The father smiled tiredly and tousled his son's head. "No one will steal your fossils. Bone hunters have some honor. Isn't that right?" He looked up at Daniel.

"Well, there have been troubles between Marsh and Cope. Just like any field, I suppose. Someone gets greedy."

"I'll shoot 'em, right between the eyes!"

Daniel hid his smile behind the napkin as he wiped his mouth. Touching his hat, he rose and picked up his pack.

It was cool outside, but he had a feeling he was late. He paused by the Ingram's cabin and knocked on the door, half expecting no one to answer, but the door opened to reveal Elizabeth.

"Mr. Bridger! You just missed Father. He got up early to go out to the site."

"Damn. I will try to catch up with him."

"Whenever you get there you'll be a great help to

them. Father talked of your talent with excavating."

"Oh, well, nothing to you, I am sure."

"Not to hear him talk! It's good that he has someone he can trust to work on the finer bones."

Suddenly he felt uncomfortable. He knew quite well that she shouldn't trust him.

"Have you eaten? There are some potatoes and sausage left over."

His stomach gurgled, not quite settled from the watery gruel. "I can't. Mrs. Goode had something prepared this morning."

She smiled, her fine lips parting over white teeth. "I can only imagine, I have heard of her meals."

He chuckled. "Yes, well. I ate anyway and could not stomach any further food."

"All right. I will send you the leftovers in case you get hungry as you go." Her skirt swished as she spun on her heel and quickly packed the contents of an iron skillet into a small pail and covered it.

His fingers brushed hers as she handed it to him. Electricity jolted through him, and his heart beat faster. He could see her holding her breath, and wondered if she felt it as well. She dropped her gaze and looked down at the pail.

"Anyway, I won't keep you. Father is waiting."

He nodded, unable to think of something more than to say, "Thank you."

Once he had left, all kinds of things burst into his mind by way of conversation. Why was he so dang-blasted tongue-tied around her? The gods that be knew he had experience enough talking with young women. But then, Elizabeth was unlike most women.

****

41

He had walked for perhaps twenty minutes when a shadow fell across him. Something struck him from behind and he tripped forward into the gravelly dirt, sharp rocks bit into his hands. Two more shadows appeared, moving too fast for him to make out any features as they struck him repeatedly with kicks to his body and face.

It stopped, and the only sound was his breath bubbling through the blood and foam in his mouth and nose. He strained to open his swelling eyes, only to see the face of Will Gunn mere inches from his.

"Mr. Wilke hopes you do not double-cross him, or it will be worse next time."

One more kick emphasized the words, and then the ground crunched as three pairs of boots moved away. Daniel lay for a moment, taking stock of his injuries. Bloodied face and nose, but most of the blows had been aimed at his arms and legs, his pack protecting his back from any attack. He made to push himself up, and nearly collapsed with pain.

Breathing slowly, he forced himself to a sitting position and looked around, dazed. He spat out some blood and dug out a handkerchief to hold to his nose. His hands bled from where he had fallen, and he knew he was in need of some aid, but his thoughts were addled from the blows that had struck him to the head.

He pulled himself up using a nearby boulder, and stood swaying uncertainly for a moment. Instinctively he headed back toward Matson, one painful step after another.

Chapter Five

Elizabeth stood by the rain barrel, washing the potatoes and parsnips. She hoped to get the stew simmering before she went to the museum to work on the oreodont some more. The potatoes in this bag had been particularly dirty and she scrubbed at them trying to get them clean. A movement caught her eye and she looked up, then screamed at the sight.

Daniel Bridger, bowed and bloodied, shambled toward her and she lifted her skirt to rush toward him. Hooking her shoulder under his arm, she helped him toward the house. After taking off his pack, she set it down as he settled into a chair with a groan. She ran to the back, pulled some rags from the rag basket and grabbed the ewer and bowl. When she reached him, it was to find him with his head leaning over the back of the chair.

"Mr. Bridger, stay awake."

He groaned again and made an effort to straighten and lift his head. She dampened a rag and began clearing the congealing blood and grit from his face. As she worked, she exposed reddened areas that were already beginning to bruise and swell. One eye was nearly swollen shut and she laid a damp, cool rag over it.

His hands were a mess as well, and it took her some time to wash the sand free from the scrapes and cuts. When he was clean, she ripped up an old sheet to make bandages for his hands and wrists. Then she sat back and observed him.

"Who did this to you?"

He shook his head and winced. "There were three of them. That man Gunn was one of them. I didn't see the other two."

"I bet it was that Rufus Howell. He did threaten us."

"I don't know. They sounded rough, but I barely saw them."

"At least your nose has stopped bleeding. There's a cut on your forehead, though, and it has me worried. Would you like some water?"

"Anything stronger?"

She retrieved a mug from the mantle and poured some rum that her mother kept as medicinal into it. Then, she held it to his lips so he could drink. He sipped, then reached up to take the cup with his bandaged hands.

"Are you feeling dizzy?"

"A little, but it is fading."

"We should get you to Mrs. Goode's house."

"I left there this morning. I was going to stay at the fossil site."

She bit her lip, and her gaze fell upon his pack. "I'll make up your bedroll on the couch, by the fire. You can stay with us until you are well enough to join them out there."

"No, I won't put you out."

"Nonsense! Where can you go like this? You will stay here, Mr. Bridger."

He winced, possibly from the force of her words.

"You remind me of my mother—I never dared disobey her." He smiled, rather lopsidedly, and she chuckled.

"She sounds like quite the matriarch."

"That she is. I'm afraid I dropped the pail of potatoes and sausage in the attack."

"Don't worry about it. I can get you some bread and cheese when you are ready."

"I'm sorry to be a burden."

"It is no trouble, though I will have to get the stew going and finish my chores."

"Don't let me stop you. I am quite comfortable...well, as much as I am capable of being. My head does spin from time to time."

She lifted the cloth to check the cut on his forehead. It had stopped bleeding, so she removed the rag, only to find his gaze fastened upon her. Her heart thumped and jumped into her throat, and she swallowed against the sensation. Ducking her head, she rose and headed back outside.

The potatoes were scattered where she had dropped them and she bent to gather them. She finished scrubbing them in the pan, then tipped the dirty water out and rinsed it before adding the vegetables and carrying it back into the house.

A glance at Daniel showed he still sat with his head tilted back. His breathing sounded easier now, and she hoped his face would not swell even more. Using her knife, she cut up the potatoes, parsnips, and their last onion.

When she had added the cut-up piece of beef she had purchased two days before from the butcher, she hooked the pan onto the arm and pushed it over the fire. Then she stole another look at Daniel.

The bruising had worsened, and blood had seeped through the bandages on his wrists and hands. Her fingers felt along his forehead for any further swelling. When she glanced down, it was to find his eyes open.

She gasped and started backward, but he grasped her hand.

"Miss Ingram, don't let me stop you."

"I can see you're well. The bleeding has stopped."

"Mmm. My head spins from time to time. Perhaps some more rum?"

"I think you should have some water, instead. Let me get you something to eat."

She turned away to cover her confusion and quickly set a plate with bread and cheese on the table beside him, then poured him some water into a mug. Her hand shook a little as she set it down.

He sighed, then reached for her hand and brought it to his bruised lips. They brushed the back of her hand and her breath caught in her throat. The world stopped as their gazes met. He let her hand go, the unbruised side of his mouth crooking upward.

"If you say anything, I will simply claim my brain was injured in the attack."

She smiled slowly. "Then I shan't say anything."

Her skirts swirled as she moved suddenly to go about her chores and cover her confusion. Without knowing what she was doing, she grabbed a rag and began dusting the main room of the cabin while she tried to remember what it was she had planned to get done. Never had a man been able to dismantle her poise so thoroughly as this one. Desperately she tried to calm her mind and remember what it was she needed to do.

Bread. That was it. She needed to bake some bread

and sweep out the cabin. She picked up her apron and pinned, then tied it in place. Her mind swirled as her hands flew, gathering the ingredients and mixing them, then kneading the dough. She left it on the bread board with a towel over it to rise and went outside to scrub the flour from her hands and forearms.

She checked on Daniel as she went past, and by the soft sound of his slow breathing, determined he was sleeping. She swept the floor, with one eye on him as she went. Foremost in her brain was the question—who had done this to him and why?

Was her father safe? Were any of the crew safe? Or was Daniel simply not telling her everything? She glanced toward him to find him staring at her. Well, one eye was open while the other was swollen shut by this time.

"You're awake."

He pushed up from the chair and leaned forward, grimacing. "Mmm. Everything's stiffening up."

She set down the broom and went to his side. Satisfied he wasn't bleeding again, she sat back on her heels and looked at him. "The bruising is truly awful. Let's make you a bed on the couch. I'm sure you need to lie down."

"I think you're right."

She unhitched the bedroll from his pack and spread it out on the seat of the wooden bench, glad she had made a pad for it the year before. He leaned heavily on her as she helped him over, but the way he was moving made her think his ribs were broken as well.

"I should call a doctor."

He grabbed her wrist, held it tightly and said, "No. No one must know."

"But how do we keep you secret? Someone will see you."

"I'll stay here a day or so until I am steadier, then I'll go to the site and remain there until I am healed. The boys will keep quiet."

"But you might be truly hurt. I must call the doctor."

"Please, Miss Ingram. Trust me. This is for the best."

The entreaty in his eyes and voice overrode her common sense and she nodded. His thumb stroked her wrist as he let her go and she spread his blanket over him.

"I have a spare pillow, I'll get it for you."

She all but ran to her father's room and picked it up, glancing in the small mirror over his wash stand. There was a smear of flour across her nose which she wiped off immediately and sighed. If only she was graceful and elegant as Charlotte Janney. The belle of Matson high society was known for her beauty and poise.

She carried the pillow back to the main room and helped Daniel arrange it under his head. He sighed as he leaned back.

"Ah. That's better. Thank you, Miss Ingram."

"Not at all."

She stirred the stew, then checked on the bread. It had finished rising so she kneaded it again and shaped it, fitting it into the Dutch oven. Then she set it to rise again beside the fire. It was too late to air the mattresses as she had planned. It would just have to wait. Instead, she took the two rugs outside to beat, then had to wash the dust from her face and arms. With a damp towel, she wiped her hair and dress down and went inside.

Daniel was attempting to stand, and she rushed forward.

"What are you doing?"

"I have need of your outhouse. I don't think you want to help me with that."

"Er…no. But I can make sure you get there safely."

"My pride says no…but my body agrees. Lead on and I will lean on you."

He kept one hand on her shoulder as she walked slowly. His left leg was stiff, and she surmised he had received a sound kick or two there. By the time they reached the small, wooden house, his breathing was short and harsh, speaking eloquently of his pain. He entered and shut the door.

She noted some boards that Silent Jim had scavenged for her chicken hutch and went over to stack them neatly. A spider crawled out. She shrieked and dropped the board in surprise. The door to the outhouse clattered open and Daniel stood there, holding his britches up.

"What happened? Are you all right?"

"Yes, sorry. There was a spider…"

He finished tucking in his shirt and securing the suspender. "Does the spider need to die, or can it go about its business?"

She laughed, breathily. "It's fine. I don't know why I acted like that. I think I'm on edge with what happened to you."

She went to his side so he could lean on her, but he merely limped beside her. "I can do this, I think I will simply look worse than I feel."

"The bruising will fade. I worry about your ribs

and your kidneys…"

"The kidneys are working fine. My pack saved them from the attack. My ribs are another matter, however."

"What can we do for them?"

"Nothing. A doctor would tell you the same. Rest, but that is all."

By this time he had reached the bench and sat upon it. She stirred the stew and pulled the little side table over closer to him, then refilled his cup.

"Are you hungry?"

"A little."

"Let me get you a plate of cheese and an apple."

"I'm sorry to be a burden…"

She smiled at him. "You're no burden. I'm enjoying the company, actually."

"Truly?"

"Of course. I'm alone so much of the time. It is a luxury to have someone to talk to."

"I should have thought you enjoyed being alone."

Her head tilted to one side as she considered. "I do, but I enjoy unobtrusive company, I suppose."

"Such as a man beaten half to death."

"If you want…Yes."

The shadows had lengthened, Elizabeth raked some coals out onto the hearth and set the Dutch oven over them, then scooped out more to pile onto the lid.

"Father will be home soon. Who knows when Ma will arrive?"

"I hope they will not mind my presence. I could ask Mrs. Goode…"

"No, no you are most welcome. Besides, you intimated that you wanted this kept from the townsfolk."

"That is true."

"Well then, it is best if Mrs. Goode knows nothing about it."

The sun must have settled over the mountain, for it darkened suddenly outside. Elizabeth spent a few minutes lighting some candles. Footsteps sounded on the porch and she spun in time to see her father come in through the door. He dropped his hat on the hook by the door and let his pack fall to the floor below it. Elizabeth winced to see dirt spread out from the spot on her clean floor.

"Successful day, Lizzie! We have cleared the overburden where we suspect the skull to be. Tomorrow may be the day—if we can get you and Mr. Bridger out there. Speaking of which, he never showed today."

"No, sir. I was attacked on my way and barely made it back in time."

Ingram noticed Daniel and started. "Good God, man! What happened to you?"

"I fear there are some who do not want me working with you."

Elizabeth frowned a little at this. It was more information than he had given her, and she wondered. It was a small thing, and yet…

Ingram peered closely at Daniel. "They got you good, man. How are your ribs?"

"Sore. May have one or two broken, but there's nothing to be done with them."

"Was Dr. Pirie called?"

"Mr. Bridger refused to see a doctor. He doesn't want his condition known in Matson."

"But…why?"

"I don't want the men behind this to have the advantage. I intend to go back to the dig and stay there. In a day or two, at least."

"Certainly, certainly, though that will extend the time before we reach the skull." He turned to Elizabeth. "We had a visitor, today. I hope it had nothing to do with what happened to Mr. Bridger."

"Oh? What happened?"

"Rufus Howell came with a proposition from Wilke to buy the claim out from under me. I told him what he could do with his offer and sent him off. Fellow had the audacity to laugh at me."

"Father, maybe we should let them have it, before more men are attacked…or worse."

"Nonsense, girl, now that I've made it clear we aren't interested, they'll go away."

Elizabeth caught Daniel's gaze. Neither one of them had much confidence in her father's proclamation. The door opened, and Mrs. Ingram came in.

"Oh Lord, love and bless us. The little girl lives. For now, anyway. We don't know about her lungs yet but for now she lives. I think I may stay home this evening."

"That's wonderful news, Ma."

Mrs. Ingram cupped Elizabeth's cheek with her hand as she moved past, then paused, and turned to see Mr. Bridger. "What on earth happened to that young man?"

Daniel repeated what he had told Dr. Ingram and she quickly checked him over, "You made nice work of these bandages, Lizzie."

"Thank you, Ma."

"Did you use a cool compress on that eye?"

"Yes, Ma."

"Did you flush out the wounds with cool water?"

"Yes, Ma."

Satisfied, Mrs. Ingram settled back and sat at the table. Elizabeth handed her a plate and spoon and dished her up some of the stew.

Dinner was quiet. Daniel's mouth was swollen, making it difficult for him to eat. Her father read a letter, choosing odd sections to read aloud though they made little sense to the three listeners.

"…'and furthermore the compound proves useful in the protection of bare bone'…well, I thought it might, but how will we know how long it will last…whatever are they using it on that for? Listen to this, 'a mixture of alcohol and…' but what of methyl acetyl?"

Elizabeth's mind wandered to the mystery of the man seated across from her. He had given up trying to eat and was leaning back, his eyes struggling to stay open as he listened to her father. Suddenly those eyes were upon her and she looked away, but saw his mouth crook up on its good side.

"I fear I am not much company tonight. I think I shall lie down if you don't mind," he said.

"Not at all."

Elizabeth stood and collected their plates. She set the lid on the pot and the Dutch oven—the leftovers would make a good breakfast. By the time she had washed up from supper and swept the hearth clean, slow, even breaths came from Mr. Bridger, though a light still flickered in her parents' room.

She climbed to the loft and set her candle down on

the little dressing table. She sighed as the clothes and corset all fell away, only to be gathered and placed on their respective hooks. When she stood in nothing but her chemise, she peeled back the covers of her bed and slipped in.

The cold sheets felt delicious to her legs, despite the chill that ran up her spine. It felt good to be free of all encumbrances for the moment and she lay on her back, staring at the ceiling overhead. The thin moonlight straggled in through the single, small window and she rolled over to stare out, chin on her hands, for a moment. In her mind she ran over all the things she would need to do the next day. Going out to the dig site was no longer an option, despite her father's hopes of getting the skull out soon.

But it would be some days before Daniel was strong enough to make it out to the site, too.

Chapter Six

Daniel's head throbbed, as did just about every part of him. Pain and stiffness met him as he awoke the next morning to the sounds of Mrs. Ingram cooking. A groan escaped him as he pushed himself up, and he fought the sudden dizziness.

Head in hands, he sat for a moment registering all the injuries that had been done to him. He stood, and suddenly Elizabeth was there supporting him. Her capable hands steadied him as he got his bearings. He broke away reluctantly to head outside.

The cool air felt good to his bruised body. Tentative fingers explored his face. At least now he could see a little out of the right eye; the swelling must have gone down. The cut on his forehead would leave a nasty scar, but then it might give him a swashbuckling air. He winced as his fingers found the bridge of his nose, which was almost certainly broken. He sighed; perhaps it wouldn't be so bad once it healed…

By the time he had washed up and gone back in, Dr. Ingram was seated at the table and Elizabeth set a plate of sliced bread and the warmed pot of stew on the table. Dr. Ingram helped Daniel fill his plate, then spread some butter on a slab of bread for him. Elizabeth placed a cup of cider in front of him and he tried to smile at both of them.

He ate slowly, taking small bites as his mouth

would not open very wide. Before he had finished half his plate, Dr. Ingram was on his way out the door, pack on his back, and rock hammer swinging at his side.

"Mr. Bridger, heal up; we need you out there."

He sighed and leaned back. "Thank you again, Miss Ingram."

"Of course. Today I have to work in the museum for a while, so you will be alone. Ma has already left to go check on the Warshadt girl. I am expecting her home at any moment. Hopefully you will be able to simply rest while I am gone."

"Is there a book or a journal I could read?"

"Oh yes! There is a bookcase in Father's room. Help yourself."

"Thank you, I will. Are there any of Dr. Ingram's papers in there?"

"A few, though Father tends to extend his research to such a degree as to forget to actually write it up. So, for the last two papers I wrote them first and he went through and corrected them. Then he sent them off."

"So you actually wrote them?"

"No, no. I simply put down in words what he had said over and over. When I wasn't sure, I would ask a question, and there would be another paragraph or two. It was really quite easy."

"Still, your name should be on them…"

"That won't happen, as you well know. But I know the part I played in my father's research, and that is enough."

She gathered the empty plates and spoons as she spoke and set them in the bucket before heading outside to wash them. He watched the door for a few moments longer, thinking.

He had feelings for this girl, he knew, and that was complicating things. He had a job to do, and he was quickly changing his mind about his alliance. Still, his neck was in a noose and he wasn't sure how he was going to get out of it…

His feet carried him to Dr. Ingram's room where the bookcase stood. An impressive collection of books were there, including a few by Darwin himself. He picked up *On the Origin of Species* and flipped through the tome. He had read it, of course, while at university, but it wouldn't hurt to review it. Rifling through the journals, he found one with a paper by W. E. Ingram and carried it and the book to his makeshift cot.

Elizabeth came in, carrying the now clean dishes and iron pot. The Dutch oven still held the remains of the bread and sat on the table with its lid in place. She bustled about, putting things away and wiping others down, before removing her apron and hanging it on the hook beside the cupboard.

"I'll be back for luncheon. Make yourself at home. She refilled his cup with water from the ewer and swished out the front door.

The house felt empty with her gone and he sat for a moment, feeling the heaviness of it. Little sounds startled him, and he knew there was a splinter of fear in him as a result of the attack. What was to stop them from coming back? Thoughts swirled around and emptied his brain…

He woke. The journal had fallen from his hand onto the floor and it was difficult to pin down where and when he was. It took a moment before reality caught up with him, and he remembered he had been attacked and was now in the Ingrams' cabin. The pounding in his head made it difficult to catch up with the present.

After drinking some water and a trip to the outhouse, he felt better…at least he felt less pain with each movement. But now he needed to find a way to get back to the *Camarasaurus* dig site. He had work to do, from a number of perspectives.

First up, a brief but thorough snoop through whatever papers he could find. He didn't know what he was looking for, but he would know when he found it. His fingers felt clumsy, protruding from the bandages and swollen. But he went through every book, checking for loose papers and looking over every one he found. There were a few letters from colleagues, but nothing personal, mostly arguing points made in his journal articles. Suddenly he heard the boards creaking from the front porch and snatched up a book to carry out.

Elizabeth closed the front door just as he limped out of Dr. Ingram's room.

He held up the book. "Always wanted to know more about the *Distribution and Evolution of North American Leporidae.*"

"Yes, rabbits and hares are fascinating from an anatomical and behavioral perspective." She glanced at the book and her gaze flicked into her father's room as she passed.

"Have you read this?"

"Of course. I found the basic premise interesting, though I am not sure I agree with the author's conclusions."

He looked down at the book. "Humph. Rather lessens my desire to read it."

"No, no you should. The information is sound…I

just wish I could sit with the author and ask a few questions. That is all."

"All right, then." He hefted the book. "I am feeling better. Can I help you?"

"No, I'm just going to slice up some bread and cheese for our luncheon."

He sat at the table, setting the book aside as she deftly cut the bread and cheese and set it before him. "We'll just eat family style if you don't mind."

"Not at all. How goes the work at the museum?"

"It goes well. I have nearly freed the zygomatic arch on the left side."

"Excellent. When do you go back to the dig?"

She sighed. "Not for a couple days. I must do laundry sometime, and then go over our accounts and see about paying the general store. Father is too wrapped up in the site to do it himself, and Ma is always out and about ministering to others."

"Can I help in any way?" he asked before he could stop himself.

"No. As I said, much of it is Father's responsibility, but I can't wait any longer for him to handle it. The general store must be paid, and I need to secure some chickens." She lifted her hands and let them fall. "So, the accounts must be gone over. And, of course, the oreodont skull needs further work. And I need to set aside a day for laundry."

He considered. There was really nothing he could do except recover enough to get out from under her feet and back out to the site where he needed to be. Too much was riding on it—not that he needed reminding. The bruises and cuts all over his body were a testament to that.

He forced himself to read and rest. Neither was to his liking as he preferred action to inaction. It was one reason he had always loved paleontology—there was a surfeit of work to be done during the season, and even over the winter.

Elizabeth went about her business. She was making something and lining a pie pan with it. After chopping up some lamb and cutting up an onion, she cooked both in a skillet over some coals, then added it to the pie pan along with some diced vegetables then covering it with more crust. This was placed in the Dutch oven and covered in coals to bake.

Once again he looked at the page beneath his fingers. He could not have recited a single fact from it. He started at the beginning and this time was able to focus on the words.

After a while, his head began to hurt and he leaned back to close his eyes. As sick and sore as he felt, he didn't know why he found it so difficult to sleep. Just then, the door opened and Mrs. Ingram came in, divesting herself of shawls and bags.

"I stopped at the general store. There's going to be an actual butcher in town in a week or so. Ol' Jensen who's been cutting the meat for the store is setting up his own place. It's going to be next to the bakery and he said he'll be getting even more kinds of meat and cuts in."

"That will be handy. Another shop to visit while out," Elizabeth said.

"I know. Glad that something will fill that space now, since the Simpsons left town…"

She came and bent over him, examining his forehead and nose. "That scar and that nose will give you quite the dashing air. How are you feeling?"

"Better. I should be going out to the dig site…"

"None of that. You'll stay here until you are well enough to go."

Elizabeth caught his eye and quirked her mouth up on one side. "Can't go against my Ma, Mr. Bridger. She won't allow it."

He smiled. Maybe he would have to stay a while longer…

****

The morning was warmer than Daniel had expected. He had been at the Ingrams for three days, and now he was on his way to the site. He stretched and ignored the shafts of pain that shot through his body with each movement. Common sense told him he needed another day or two resting and recuperating, but he could not continue to be around Elizabeth and not put his job in jeopardy.

The ground crunched beneath his boots and long-stemmed grass slashed at his legs. It was still difficult to breathe through his nose, and so he kept his mouth open as he walked. By the time they reached the point where he had been attacked, his whole body was complaining and he had no way of easing the pain.

Unprepared for the emotions that coursed through him, he scanned the hills around them and licked his lips. There were no shadows approaching today—only the broad back of Dr. Ingram pulling farther away. He hurried to catch up and ended up nearly treading on the man's heels. He eased off and maintained a place a few feet behind him on the path.

They arrived in camp before the makeshift sundial read nine. Dr. Ingram went immediately to gauge the progress towards the head of the fossil and Daniel lowered himself slowly to the section of neck he had been working on. He looked up to find four gazing at him and he explained what had happened up to the point where one attacker had whispered to him. That, he was keeping to himself. Their expressions shifted from interest to shock as he talked.

"Are we all in danger, boss?" Henry asked.

"Now boys, don't take on. I'm sure we're all safe enough," Ingram said.

"I'm not getting beat up for no bones."

"Me either."

"Now hang on, no one's going to get beat up…"

"He did!"

"And we don't know why."

Again, his fingers felt clumsy as he tried to grasp the chisel and hammer. "I don't know what they wanted. Maybe they were some of Cope's or Marsh's men thinking I was working for the other. They didn't say so I don't know."

"We'll just keep on working quietly and leave the other teams alone."

"You think Wilke was behind it?"

"Surely he wouldn't stoop to such tactics," Ingram said. "No, I think it was a misguided attempt to discourage the work in general, for some unknown reason. We just need to keep our heads down and travel in teams. Now, let's get to work."

Daniel worked away for a while, his fingers eventually becoming less stiff the more he worked them. When the day heated up, he curled up in the shadow of the embankment and rested his aching head for a while. The other men left him alone and he found himself thinking of Elizabeth and wondering what she was doing.

He fell asleep, waking up disoriented again with his body sore where the rocky ground had pressed into him. He could see the other three and Dr. Ingram seated around the fire, eating. Shadows had spread from the west and covered much of the ground. He pushed up slowly, aching everywhere and stumbled over to the fire.

Henry moved over, making room for him on the log and he nodded his thanks. Dr. Ingram looked up and smiled.

"Ah! You're awake. I must say I was glad to see you take your rest when you needed it."

"You should have wakened me. I have work to do."

"It will get done. I know I push you boys, but if you are injured, there is nothing more you can do." He glanced at the sky and added, "I need to get home."

"You shouldn't walk alone," Daniel said.

"I should be fine. I'll keep my rock hammer ready."

"Sir, let me accompany you."

"Daniel, you are in no condition to be walking that distance repeatedly. Besides, I understood that you wished to remain hidden while you healed."

"I hate this, though."

Dr. Ingram left, waving off the offers of company from the other men. Silent Jim handed Daniel a piece of flatbread and some jerky. He ate automatically, trying not to wince at the pain in his face with every chew. The third man, named Charlie, handed him a mug of fresh water from the creek and he drank it gratefully.

"Any sign of the skull?" he asked.

Three heads shook. "Got some overburden removed though," Morty said.

"We are nearly to the depositional layer now. We should get close tomorrow," Silent Jim muttered softly.

The men fell silent. In the distance, an owl hooted, his call echoing off the rocky walls. The stars had begun to come out as the sky darkened. Henry picked up a guitar and began playing quietly while Charlie whittled and Jim stared off into the distance. Daniel felt himself falling asleep and quickly made up his bedroll and laid down. His thoughts were scattered, and he had difficulty focusing on anything except Elizabeth.

****

A train thundered toward him, its whistle blaring as he stood captured by its great mouth, which suddenly transformed into a Tyrannosaurus skull. He jerked awake, but the sound continued.

He looked over to where it was coming from, only to see Henry kneeling on the ground, howling out in a panic-stricken voice. He went to the man and shook him, and Henry gasped, pointing at the ground.

Following his finger, Daniel gazed upon a horrific scene. Blood pooled in the sand, darkening as it congealed. Silent Jim lay silent in death, his throat cut and his eyes half-closed as though he had been killed while awakening.

Realization struck him hard, stunning him. Silent Jim had been killed, while they all slept. Had someone sneaked into camp and struck him down, or was it one of them?

Charlie stared at him with an ugly look and Henry pointed at him now. "You did this. We were safe until you came."

"Look at me! Do I look like I could kill someone?"

"Didn't take much effort—just a jab and a flick of a sharp knife," Charlie said.

Henry now looked at Charlie. "You seem to know an awful lot about it."

But Daniel examined the ground around Jim and the camp. "There's footsteps coming from this direction. It looks like someone snuck in and killed the first man he found. The question is...why?"

"I'll tell you why—to scare us off the site. And it worked. I'm leaving," Henry said as he rolled up his blankets and tied them to his pack.

"Now wait a minute. Dr. Ingram will be here soon, we can find out what needs to be done. The sheriff may need to talk to you, Henry. To all of us. But someone needs to go inform him."

"I'll go, with Dr. Ingram when he gets here— unless he's been attacked and killed, too."

The gravel on the path crunched and Dr. Ingram appeared, swinging his hammer and humming tunelessly. He stopped when he caught sight of the three men. Daniel looked at him, then pointed toward Silent Jim.

Ingram paled and recoiled. "What's happened? Why is there blood? What is going on?"

"Jim was struck down while he slept. None of us woke up or saw anything."

Ingram stared. Daniel tried to intercept his gaze.

"We need to contact the sheriff. Do you know if Jim had any family?"

Shaking his head, he dragged his gaze away from the grisly site. "We need to get his body back to town."

Charlie took his hatchet and went to some tall saplings to cut them down. Once they were stripped, he lashed them together at one end and used Jim's blanket to build the bed of the travois. When it was finished, he brought it over to where Jim still lay and together they loaded his stiffening body onto it before covering it with another blanket.

Jim's spotted mule was brought over and the travois secured to it, then Charlie said, "Who's going with me?"

Henry stood up, and Dr. Ingram said, "I suppose I should go. That would leave Daniel here alone."

"I don't want to be here alone."

"We can't leave the site unguarded—" Ingram began.

"For God's sake, a man has been killed. Who knows if we will all be next?"

Ingram struggled internally for a moment, then he shook his head and said, "Of course, of course. We must all go into town. Gather your things, let's go."

It was a solemn procession into town. The little mule pulled slowly, and the men had to stop for Daniel a few times, but by the time the sun was overhead, they had reached the edges of town. Ingram led the way to the one room jail where the sheriff might usually be found.

Sheriff Alistair Hancock appeared in the doorway and stopped when he saw them coming toward the jail. His handsome mustache twitched and his thick eyebrows met. "Dr. Ingram. What is it?"

"We've been attacked. One of our crew is dead," Dr. Ingram said.

Hancock frowned, stepped over to the travois, and

lifted the blanket. Then he looked up at all the men. Daniel stepped forward and explained what happened. Hancock's face was inscrutable. When Daniel had finished, he asked, "And what happened to you?"

Slowly he told him of being attacked on his way to the dig site. He left off the warning that had been whispered to him, however, and he could see that the sheriff suspected him of something.

"You look about done in. Go home. Where is that by the way?"

"I…I don't know."

"You can stay with us, Bridger." Ingram looked at the other two and added, "That goes for you boys as well."

Charlie shook his head. "I'll head back to my claim. You can find me there."

Henry nodded. "Same here. Just southwest of the Travers Trail where it crosses Spitfire Creek."

Morty stood with his hands in his pockets and said, "I'll be in town. Just leave a message at the tavern." He slouched off and disappeared in the mid-day shoppers.

The sheriff turned back to Ingram. "Whose mule is this?"

Ingram nodded to the travois. "His."

The sheriff sighed. "Might as well sell it to Riggs to pay for the coffin."

Daniel turned to follow Ingram toward the cabin on the edge of town. The others had scattered, and he still wasn't sure what he felt about everything. He simply went along with the flow of things for the moment.

Elizabeth looked up with surprise from the large tub she was stirring next to the laundry line. "Father? Mr. Bridger?" She followed them inside where they divested themselves of their packs.

With a sigh of exhaustion, Ingram repeated the story of what had happened. Daniel sat and willed his spinning head to stop. He found a cup of cider placed in his hands and he drank it down, then leaned his head back. Gentle fingers probed the wound on his forehead and he opened his eyes.

"Well?"

"It is healing well. Your nose is still swollen, however."

"Yes. It hurts to breathe."

"You have done too much. You need to rest." Her hazel eyes were soft with concern.

He shook his head. "Your father is spent, though he will not admit it."

Her head turned to her father, who sat slumped in a chair by the fire. Her hand fell on his shoulder. "Father, are you all right?"

"Poor Silent Jim! Alone in the world and then this happens! And the *Camarasaurus*—there is no one to protect her."

"Father, lives are at stake. First Mr. Bridger, now Jim. We must let it go."

He shook his head. "Never. I will fight this."

"We can fight it together, but not today," Daniel said.

Dr. Ingram lifted his head to stare at him, then nodded. "I appreciate that, Mr. Bridger. We must present a solid front to these men. But, oh…poor Jim!"

Elizabeth wiped away a tear and nodded. "But Father, don't take on so…remember your heart."

He patted her on the shoulder and then buried his face in his hands.

Chapter Seven

Not since her brother's death had Elizabeth seen her father look so defeated. She tightened her grip on his forearm momentarily, but had to get back to the laundry. The water might have boiled away by now.

It hadn't. The fire had died down to embers while unattended and she spent a few minutes feeding it and raising it up from the ashes. After twisting the water from the clothes, she hung them on the line and then sluiced clean, cold water over her arms and dried them on her apron. She added it to the line, and then went into the house to figure something out for supper.

Her father had not moved, but Daniel was staring into the fire. He looked up as she came in and she once again felt that spark ignite. Did he feel it too?

"Can I do anything?" he asked.

"No, just rest. You've had a wretched day. I am so shocked for dear Jim. He never hurt a soul."

"Life is not always fair, and the people responsible for this have much to answer for," her father said.

"Father, go lie down. You must think of your heart murmur."

"I am well, Elizabeth. But maybe you are right. I am feeling done in."

He pushed himself heavily to his feet and stumbled into his room. The bed creaked and the mattress rustled as he lay down. She looked down at her fingers, then up at Daniel.

"I didn't know your father had heart trouble."

She shrugged. "The doctor has told him repeatedly not to push himself, but you see what he is like when it comes to bones."

"Daughter of bones…" he said softly.

"What was that?"

He shook his head. "Just my fanciful way of referring to you."

"I don't know how I feel about that. I think I like it."

He chuckled. "You should. It was intended to be complimentary."

She stood. "I must go to the store to get something for supper. I'll be back." She lifted the basket beside the door and went out before he could say anything. Her cheeks felt hot, and she hoped he had not noticed.

The air had warmed outside and she was sweating a little by the time she reached the store. She loaded some potatoes into her basket and looked up as a shadow passed over her. Rufus Howell stood there gazing earnestly down at her.

"Miss Ingram! This is a delight!"

"Mr. Howell, how do you do?"

"Quite well! I'm here supervising the food for our camp."

"Oh yes?" She hoped she sounded polite.

"Yes, such a chore, but the workers must be fed. I'm sure you face the same problem."

"Well, my father handles that, so…"

"Oh of course. Though I understand you are quite involved in your father's work."

"Yes, naturally. I find it all so fascinating."

"Whereas laundry and baking are not?"

"Perhaps not rivetingly so, but I do not mind them."

He smiled, and yet his face had an unpleasant expression to it. As though he secretly looked down on her and simply humored her with words.

She reached for some carrots and said, "Excuse me, I must get a soup going."

"Yes, I had heard your father was back in town. And that something had happened out at the dig. Poor Mr. Bridger is said to look much the worse for it."

Her mouth dropped open, but no sound came out. "Excuse me," she said and edged around him to go to the counter where she requested a roast and a piece of ham. "Oh, and some bacon while you are at it."

"How is your flour?" Mrs. Hutchins, the wife of the store owner, asked.

"It's fine for now. Getting a little low on lard, though, and probably need some corn meal and a small jar of honey."

Elizabeth could feel Mr. Howell's gaze upon her as he settled with Mr. Hutchins and left. She let loose a sigh, and wondered where he had gotten his information. Was it already common knowledge that a murder had taken place at their site? How long before Howell and the rest of Wilke's crew took over the site?

She hurried home. Her father's snores echoed from his bedroom and Mr. Bridger lay stretched out on his couch. He rose, however, and took the basket from her. He carried it to the table and she filled her apron with some vegetables to carry out to the rain barrel and wash. When she got back, she pulled out the knife and cutting board to begin assembling a soup for supper. He sat at the table and watched her.

"You do that so easily. Where did you learn to handle a knife like that?"

She laughed. "My mother taught me after my brother died to keep me from fretting about it."

"When did he die?"

"Eight years ago. He caught diphtheria and could not recover, no matter what we did."

"You sound as though you feel guilty over it."

"I do, a little. And I know Father wonders if there was something else we could have done. He had fallen asleep tending him when he slipped away."

"But, I've heard from others that loved ones often wait until moments such as that to finally pass."

"Yes, I've heard that as well. We buried him in the churchyard. I usually go on Sundays."

Elizabeth focused for a moment on slicing the bit of beef and the vegetables. A little lard in the cooking pot and she could quickly brown the beef and onions before adding water and vegetables to simmer for a while. Soon, the cabin was filled with the smells of beef and vegetable soup.

After cleaning off the table and washing it down, she looked up to find his gaze upon her. "I'm sorry we are not more entertaining."

"Nonsense. I'm very entertained."

Her cheeks grew hot suddenly and she looked down at her hands. Lifting her gaze abruptly she said, "How are you feeling? In pain?"

"Uh, yes, but I'm much improved."

"Good. I have a feeling Father is going back out to the site as soon as possible. This afternoon, perhaps."

"Alone?"

"If I can't dissuade him."

The door to the bedroom opened and Dr. Ingram came out, running a hand through his thinning hair. "What say you, Bridger, are you up for going out to the dig site?"

"Father, no. It is much too dangerous."

"Can't be helped, Little Bit. Wilke's crew could be there already."

"Didn't the sheriff say to stay in town while they investigated?"

"He will know where to find us if he needs us. At any rate, we must head back."

"Well, I'm going with you."

Both men looked up at her. "You can't. We mean to stay."

"Then I will stay."

"But you can't, you are a female."

"It is no more than pioneer women do. You know I am one of your best excavators."

"But, the laundry...the cooking. What will you do?"

"I will have to come back every few days to wash, I suppose. Ma is here, and she can handle things by herself for a little while. By then you may have acquired a new crew."

"Elizabeth, no. You will have to sleep on the ground in the open."

"Father, I am determined."

"Mr. Bridger, help me convince her it is wrong."

But Daniel's brown eyed gaze was fixed upon her and he said after a moment, "I am inclined to agree with Miss Ingram. If that is truly what she wants, then who am I to deny her?"

Her father simply looked from one to another. Finally, he shrugged. "I have never been able to tell you no, Elizabeth. We must get ready to go."

She sighed. "Father, can we leave in the morning?"

"We may already be too late. Squatters may be there."

"One night, Father. That is all I ask. I have supper in the pot and Mr. Bridger could use the rest. And you are not as young as you once were."

He looked from one to the other, and his head fell onto his chest. "One night, Elizabeth. We leave at dawn, however."

"We cannot leave before Silent Jim's funeral." Daniel said.

"I will go speak to the parson, find out when that is to be." He grabbed his hat and set out, footsteps coming down a little harder than usual.

Elizabeth stirred the soup and pulled the jug of sourdough starter towards her. Minutes later she had a loaf of bread ready to bake in the Dutch oven. When she went to the cupboard for the bowls, Daniel rose and took them from her, setting the table himself. Eyebrows raised, she watched and suddenly his gaze met hers.

She didn't realize how close he was until he spun to look at her. It was only a short distance and he leaned toward her suddenly and kissed her lightly on the mouth.

Shock, rooted her to the spot. Her body responded, edging toward him and feeling his warmth as his lips played lightly with hers. He stopped, and pulled back.

"I apologize, Miss Ingram."

"I...no..." Words stumbled about in her head.

He looked stricken. "Excuse me. I'll wait outside

until your father returns."

Her mind grasped desperately to understand what had just happened. He had kissed her! But why, when he had seemed so disgusted with himself afterward. What did it all mean?

And how did she feel about being kissed?

One hand came up to lightly touch her lips where just moments before, his had been. Once the shock was over, she realized she had enjoyed her first kiss immensely. More than that, she wanted to repeat it, but first she needed to talk to Daniel about it.

Leaving supper to continue simmering, she followed him out to the porch where he stood at the end, staring off.

"Mr. Bridger?"

He spun. "Miss Ingram." His gaze met hers for only a moment before he glanced away.

"Sir, about what just happened…"

"Miss, I can only apologize."

"But you needn't…"

His gaze lifted to hers. "But…"

"We cannot go on like that, but we can continue on a slower path."

A shadow of a smile touched his lips. "Oh yes?"

"Yes." One corner of her mouth twitched upward and he smiled in response.

"I see."

They stared at one another for a moment, then Elizabeth broke off and stepped back through the open door. "Supper is ready when Father gets back."

"All right. I will wait out here until then. I need to collect myself. I hope you understand."

"I do." She closed the door softly and leaned back

against it, sighing. Her heart raced, and she could not have described what she felt, but she suspected she was in love. Though surely it was not such a violent emotion as what she felt right now...

With a corner of her apron, she carried the soup to the table and then lifted the bread from the Dutch oven. In a daze, she retrieved the butter and set it on the table as well.

Then she sat in her chair and took a deep breath to steady her nerves before Daniel, and her father came inside.

Chapter Eight

Daniel took a deep breath to settle his heartbeat. He wasn't sure how it had happened, but he thought he and Miss Ingram had decided to court. This was a complication he didn't need, and he wasn't sure what to do about it.

From the distance he could see the steeple of the church. The door opened and someone emerged. He presumed it was Dr. Ingram and he waited as the figure drew nearer. Soon enough, he was at the edge of the porch, kicking dust from his boots and stepping up.

He nodded to Daniel and went past him into the house. Daniel followed. They congregated around the table as Dr. Ingram took off his hat and ran a hand through his thinning hair.

"Funeral is set for tomorrow at eleven or so. It will be short as the parson has another funeral to attend to."

Elizabeth frowned. "Who?"

"Old Mrs. Olensky."

"Oh, poor thing, she's been addled for a long while."

"Yes, a blessing really." He sat heavily in the chair. "We can leave after luncheon tomorrow. I will spend the morning getting supplies."

"Father, how will we get them out there?"

"I will have to hire a donkey, I suppose."

"What happened to Silent Jim's mule?"

"Probably sold to pay for the funeral."

"Do we have the money for a mule?" Elizabeth asked.

"Well, I may be able to borrow one from Riggs."

"Do you want me to go ask him?" Daniel asked.

"No, no. I'll go. You can go with Elizabeth to order our supplies."

"I can do that." He smiled at Elizabeth and was rewarded with a shy smile in response.

It was quiet for a while as they ate. It was difficult not to lock gazes with her, and then it was difficult to tear his glance away. He didn't know if they would declare themselves to her father, or go on in secret. Luckily, it looked like he would have plenty of time alone with her to talk.

Soon enough supper was finished, and everyone rose to go to their assigned duties. Dr. Ingram grabbed his hat and went out, leaving Daniel alone with Elizabeth. She busied herself clearing the table and he reached out to place a hand on her arm.

"We should go to the general store."

She caught her breath and lifted her gaze to his. "Yes, I suppose so.

She took off her apron and hung it up, then turned to him. Her head was tilted at just such an angle that it took the space of a second for him to lean down and kiss her gently.

She kissed him back and his hands cupped her face. Then they traveled down to pull her close. Her mouth opened and she gasped, pulling back and he cocked his head.

"What is it?"

"I'm just…We should go."

But she didn't struggle against him. Slowly he loosened his hold, though he did not release her gaze.

"Let's go. Are we going to tell your father?"

"I think he will figure it out. He is upset enough about the situation, so let's say nothing for now."

Daniel nodded. "I will let you guide me in this."

They headed out the door and turned along the walkway toward the store. Once there, they worked together to come up with a list of supplies needed. Mr. Hutchins nodded as they spoke, making notes. Though his injuries had mostly healed, enough of the bruising remained to catch the grocer's attention.

"Heard about what happened to you. They need to catch these bastards."

"I hope they do."

"I'll have it all on the back deck ready for you to pick up tomorrow morning. You got a cart?"

"Father is borrowing a mule."

He nodded and turned away, leaving them to make their way out of the emptying store and head home in the twilight. As they walked, Daniel let his hand brush against hers, which drew her gaze up to his.

"I don't know how to do this. It's all new."

"Neither do I. We'll just have to figure it out."

She swallowed and nodded, then gave him a quick smile before she looked away. He smiled down at the top of her head and struggled against the urge to put his arm around her.

Dr. Ingram was there when they got to the cabin. He looked up from stoking the fire as they walked in and said, "Well, Riggs will loan us a mule, but we will need to bring it back within two days. I don't know how we will do that."

"I will bring it back and return to the site."

"And risk being beaten again?" Elizabeth's voice rose in concern beside him.

"I'll have a mule this time, and I'll be prepared on my way back."

Ingram sighed unhappily. "We'll have to see. Perhaps my crew will come back and we can send someone with you."

They settled around the fire. Dr. Ingram read a journal he'd received in the mail. Elizabeth mended one of her father's shirts by candlelight, and Daniel watched her. When she had finished, nipping the thread with her teeth, she picked up a dress to mend a small tear in the skirt. Her stitches were tiny and neat, and he marveled at them.

"Another skill you learned from your mother?"

She nodded. "Yes. She can sew anything. I'm afraid I would rather be outside with a rock hammer in hand, but she made sure I could handle a needle."

Soon their eyes were tired of peering through the gloom and they all went to bed. He laid on his couch, listening to the sounds of Elizabeth getting ready. The slight rustle of her dress hitting the ground and then the creak of the ropes and wood as she climbed into bed. It crossed his mind briefly that he had abandoned his real purpose, but he pushed the thought aside.

He would find a way to do it all, and somehow keep the paleontologist's daughter.

****

The shadows were short, coming from the sun overhead as they set out the next morning. The funeral had been brief, and they had been the only mourners present to see Silent Jim lowered into the earth in his box. A wooden cross with his name on it was pounded into the ground and Elizabeth laid a posy of flowers beside it.

Daniel had fetched the mule and stopped to strap all their supplies to its back. Then he slung their packs over its back as well, making sure to secure them all with rope.

"You made a fine job of that."

"Where did you learn to load a mule?" Elizabeth asked.

"Oh, a neighbor had a farm. You know how it is…" He faltered, not liking lying to the girl he loved.

Love? Is that what this was? But love led to marriage and children and…surely not? This could not be what he was doing.

What if it was? What then? It would completely upend his life and plans. There were things he was involved in that precluded attachments. And yet he could not break this off… He could not.

His hand tightened on the mule's lead rope and he flashed a look in her direction. She walked beside her father, listening as he discussed the latest paper he had read. And yet she threw him a glance that told him her mind was on him. He could not help but smile at her.

Dr. Ingram chose that moment to turn toward him. He instantly wiped the look from his face. "Daniel, how is the mule doing?"

"He's fine. I think it was Jim's mule, so this is all familiar to him. He seems to know where we're going."

"Ah, excellent. Very fitting."

Daniel peered ahead and noted a thin trail of smoke coming up from the hills in the distance. It looked like a campfire. A campfire near the *Camarasaurus* site…

Dr. Ingram saw it at the same time. "Damn it, someone's there. They've taken over my site. My dig!"

"Now, Father, there may be another explanation. Maybe it isn't our site after all…"

"It is Howell, with Wilke behind him. They've stolen my dinosaur!"

"I doubt they have hauled off any of the bones." But Dr. Ingram was dangerously red in the face and neck, and Elizabeth's voice was fearful. "We'll be there in twenty minutes or so, then we'll know."

They fell silent, as though straining through the early afternoon air to hear sounds coming from the site. Daniel listened hard for the sounds of a hammer hitting a chisel or bare rock. He heard nothing, though, save the occasional thud that might be a pickaxe loosening overburden.

The anticipation grew as they neared the site. Dr. Ingram readied his rock hammer, and even Elizabeth retrieved hers to hold at the ready. He followed suit, and they all neared the turn of the path around the outcrop together.

Dr. Ingram was in the lead, and as he went around, he stopped altogether. Then, with a rush, he ran forward, with Elizabeth trailing behind. Daniel had to wait, for the mule was dragging its feet. But when he turned the corner, Elizabeth and Dr. Ingram stood beside Henry, whose pickaxe rested beside him.

"Daniel, look who it is!"

Henry shrugged. "Nothin' goin' on at the claim. Might as well dig up bones."

Daniel grinned and waved to him, then led the mule to the stream to drink before returning to tie it to a tree. It seemed to take a long time for it to finally drink its fill and be ready to be led back to the camp. The mule tossed his head and Daniel spent a moment calming him down before starting to tie him up. He had just finished anchoring the rope to the tree when the camp went silent. He stepped out from under the tree to see Howell on horseback with a few of his crew around. All of them had guns.

A tense standoff ensued. Daniel's hand lay on the gun at his hip as he looked from Dr. Ingram to Howell, his gaze drawn to the sun glinting off the barrel of Howell's rifle. Finally, Howell spoke.

"Just came to check on your site. Make sure it's tended to and watched."

"As you can see, we have it under control," Ingram said in a loud voice.

Howell seemed to be thinking. The barrel of the rifle stayed up as he said, "I am prepared to offer you a deal. We excavate and keep the bones; you get sole access to write it up."

"I already have that, and the fossils. There is no need of a 'deal.'"

"Mr. Wilke is very insistent that he get control of this sauropod."

"Mr. Wilke will be very disappointed."

Another tense minute passed, then the rifle was lifted, and the other guns dropped as well. Howell simply nodded to Dr. Ingram, then looked straight at Daniel.

"Well, Bridger, you can come along with us, now. We don't need your services any longer."

Confusion reigned on the faces of Dr. Ingram and his daughter. Daniel's face flamed with anger and embarrassment as understanding finally dawned on them.

"Daniel...you were working for the Howell crew all along?" Dr. Ingram's hurt expression cut him to the core, but it was Elizabeth who turned angry eyes upon him.

"You...you...pirate! How dare you! I wish they'd killed you!"

He could say nothing. He simply pulled his pack down from the mule's back and walked off toward the Howell crew. Rage seethed under the surface, however. Anger at being outed in so cruel a way. It had been intended to hurt Dr. Ingram, and Daniel knew it had done so. He could not help but see the grins of the crew members as he joined them, and he whirled to make one last appeal to the Ingrams before leaving.

They were turned away from him. Howell reined his horse around and the crew headed off. Daniel lingered for a moment, but the Ingrams simply stood, backs turned so he could not see their faces.

The pressure around his heart finally reached a peak, and broke.

Chapter Nine

Daniel? A spy? Elizabeth's mind whirled beneath the angry storm. Suddenly hot embarrassment shot through her as she considered his actions in light of this new information. He had simply used her, and she had been too stupid and love blind to see it.

Her eyes smarted, and she quickly dabbed her hand against them to help stem the tears. She would not cry here, now. She would not.

Her father stood still; his shoulders hunched in near defeat. She knew what this deceit had cost him, and she was doubly angry at Daniel because of it. It was one thing to lie to her, but her father trusted so easily…

She pulled on his arm to get him to move toward the campfire and after a hesitation he came. When she was sure they were gone, she went to the mule and began untying the ropes—the ropes that Daniel had fixed only hours ago when life had been sweet and shining.

But now…

She tried not to think about it, but thoughts would intrude. Daniel had been a spy—a spy for Wilke and Howell, and now he was gone.

The knot in the rope held and she tore a fingernail trying to undo it. Pain shot through her finger and triggered the tears to fall. She kept herself turned to the pack on the mule as tears fell. The corner of her large work apron was sodden before she had control of herself.

After pulling out her knife, she cut through the bonds holding everything to the back of the mule and they fell away, one by one. Henry spread out a canvas tarp that they could put the edible items into, which would be gathered together and suspended from a tall branch. This would keep animals from getting into their food.

She moved her pack over near the rock overhang. Clouds had formed overhead, and were darkening. Like her soul.

The iron skillet pulled on her hands as she transferred it to the grate over the fire. She cut up some bacon and set it to sizzling in the skillet while she pulled a few potatoes from the sack and cut them up. Soon they were frying in the fat. As they simmered, she took the water pail and dumped out its dusty contents before taking it to the stream to refill.

By the time supper was ready, another figure had wandered down from the mountainside. Charlie appeared, pack and pickaxe in hand. Without saying a word, he set his bedroll by the fire and retrieved his metal plate, then helped himself to the potatoes and bacon. Soon, everyone was seated around the fire, eating, except Elizabeth who claimed not to be hungry.

It wasn't far from the truth, which was that food made her feel sick at the moment. When would this pain end? And yet again she wondered how Daniel could have deceived them so easily.

Charlie tossed a rope over the branch of a nearby tree. It took him a few tries, but then he and Henry were able to raise the food sack up to a safe height. The sun had disappeared in the tumult of clouds overhead, and soon the air was split by the crack of thunder.

The rain hit before they could react, but everyone caught up their pack and made for the overhang. Elizabeth's was already there, but even so she was thoroughly damp by the time she huddled up against the solid sandstone wall.

The rain poured down as the storm rumbled through the narrow valley. Lightning struck around them, sending great shock waves through the air and puffs of smoke and sand. A nearby tree writhed in heat and light for a split second, then simply steamed in the pounding rain.

The four humans huddled under the overhang. Henry spread out his bedroll and stretched out upon it. Charlie followed suit. That left only the Ingrams sitting up in the rocky alcove. Elizabeth sighed and spread her own bedroll out. She rested her head upon the rest of her pack, staring out at the sodden campsite. Water streamed down over rocks and she could hear the stream swelling.

A rock pressed painfully into her hip and she tried shifting about, but it did no good. The ground was rocky and uneven, and uncomfortable. She gave up and simply relaxed into it, and found it was a little more bearable.

Morning brought sunshine, which began drying the soaked ground. Elizabeth rose and placed the pot over the fireplace. Henry brought some wood that had been stored under the overhang and started a fire. She mixed some gruel in the iron pot and set it over the embryonic fire to start cooking. In the skillet she dropped some slices of bacon and pulled some burning tinder underneath the grate. The hem of her skirt was damp from the wet ground by the time breakfast was ready.

Her father dipped some gruel onto his plate and added a rasher of bacon to it. Elizabeth let the others fill their plates first, then filled hers. The hot food revived her, and though she still hurt from Daniel's desertion, she felt she could focus on clearing another vertebra from the rock.

Charlie and Henry went off to work on the overburden, while she and her father knelt over the drying ground to begin chiseling out the chunks of rock carrying the fossils. How they would get them back to the museum in Matson, she didn't know. Hopefully her father had some ideas.

The sandstone gave way beneath her chisel fairly easily, meaning she needed to sweep debris out of the way frequently with the small hand broom. She found the work a balm to her soul, though thoughts of Daniel were never far away. And with each thought, came pain in her heart that she didn't think would ever end.

Henry and Charlie set down their picks and collected the mule to take back to Matson. Elizabeth was a little nervous about being alone with only her father as company and the Howell crew still out there. But there was little else to be done. The mule had to be returned, and the two men were the best option for that.

She watched them leave, then turned her attention back to her work. Her father's hammer hit the chisel in a smooth rhythm born from years of practice. She suddenly realized she had stopped her work, and was simply listening.

With a decisive strike, she hit the top of the chisel, but her hammer slid off and hit the hand holding the chisel instead. It was a common occurrence amongst beginners, but she was embarrassed. And in pain. She dropped the hammer and rubbed the spot it had struck, groaning lightly.

"Ah, Little Bit, be careful."

"I know, Father. Don't know what's wrong with me." She regretted the words as soon as they were out of her mouth. It was only too obvious what was wrong with her…

The afternoon wore on, and though clouds gathered just like the day before, the storms stayed away. She began cooking another potato skillet before the men had returned. It finished as the sky was clearing. The sun sent long shadows in the dying light before Charlie and Henry returned.

Her father jumped up to greet them. "What happened? We expected you hours ago."

Charlie handed a piece of paper to him. "This was nailed to the door of the Fossil Emporium."

Wilberforce read it, his mouth a grim line.

"What is it, Father…what does it say?"

He handed her the parchment and she frowned at it.

You are ordered to vacate these premises by May 1, 1879, or forfeit all items within.

"But the only way they could do this is if you hadn't been paying rent. Have you?"

"Of course. There was that little time before Christmas when I was late with the rent, but then I sold the hadrosaur skull and all was well. Of course, in all the excitement over things, I may have forgotten to pay this month's rent, but it is only a few days…or weeks…late."

"We need to go to the mayor…"

"Old Janney may be behind this. We know Wilke is funding the Howell crew, and is good friends with the mayor."

"Then the sheriff!"

"He is paid by the mayor. No, Elizabeth. They are trying to stretch us, force us to leave this site so they can confiscate it."

"So what do we do? If we leave here, then there will only be Henry and Charlie left, and they could easily be overrun by Howell's crew. But if we don't, we will lose the museum."

Wilberforce gnawed on one of his knuckles as he stared at the ground. Elizabeth laid a hand on his shoulder. "Father, I need to go back into town. You stay here. Maybe Henry or Charlie can go out and recruit a couple more miners to come help."

"I can't send you alone. Charlie can escort you..."

"And who will escort him back? He would be just as vulnerable."

"Elizabeth—"

"No, Father. I will get my pack and head back alone. I will keep my hammer ready. You must trust me."

His mouth opened, and he looked with mute entreaty at the other men, but no one offered an argument to the plan. Elizabeth nodded, then quickly packed her things and donned her pack. She kissed her father's stubbly cheek and headed off.

Though her knees shook, she stepped quickly along the path toward Matson. A bush rattled nearby and she jumped, only to find a rabbit had startled from its hiding place. She took a deep breath and set out once more.

The quiet sounds of birds and wind through the trees gave her space to think unwelcome thoughts. Why hadn't Daniel argued against the charges? He had simply accepted them and joined the Howell crew. As though he had been expecting it for some time…

She brushed a loose lock of hair back from her face as though to wipe all thoughts of Daniel away. But he would intrude. Tears edged out the corners of her eyes and she let them fall. There was no one to see her after all.

Sooner than she expected, she passed the outskirts of the town. Stopping first at the cabin, she washed up and changed her dress. Her Ma was out, and the cabin lay empty as she cleaned up. At the last minute, she tied her Sunday bonnet on and headed out to the museum.

People stepped out of her way as she strode along, chin up. When she reached the museum, the door was open and there were men inside.

"Gentlemen, may I help you?"

The men spun around. Mayor Janney and the sheriff were among them. She let her gaze take them all in.

"Why are you here on private property? The museum is not open right now, and I know I locked the door when I left."

Mayor Janney gave her a smile that didn't reach his eyes. "A notice was posted yesterday, explaining that your father must leave the premises for non-payment. I'm surprised he is not here himself."

"He sent me in his stead."

"Alone?" his voice was incredulous.

"As you see."

"Miss, I am not accustomed to speaking with

young women about business matters."

"I run this museum in my father's name. He is preoccupied with fossil sites and acquisition. I handle everything else but the payments. However, I am prepared to do so now if there has been one missed."

Janney frowned, as though not expecting this. "With what money?"

Her eyebrows shot up. "Where money often comes from—the bank."

"I've checked..." He paused, knowing full well he should not have access to their banking records.

Her eyebrows lowered. "Sir, are you accusing me of lying?"

"No, Miss Ingram, it is just too late."

A moment passed, then her head tilted to one side. "But, sir, think how well this museum suits a town like Matson. No other town on the Front Range can boast of one. We often get visitors and school children. Surely it is worth preserving?"

Janney's mouth opened, but no sound came out. She saw his mind spinning and calculating. What she had said was true. She had often heard council members boast of Matson's museum. She knew they, at least, would support her. Would Janney go against his own council just to ingratiate himself to Stanthorpe Wilke?

He relaxed back ever so slightly, and she knew she had won... at least a partial victory.

"Do I have your word that the missing payment will be in my hands before the end of the week?"

"You have my word. I will bring it to your office myself."

His mouth worked a moment before saying, "Well then, you may stay for the present. I can't guarantee you this space indefinitely."

"All I ask is that when the time comes for us to leave, you give us proper notice,"

"Well, I am a fair man after all. You may be assured of that."

He glanced around at the men with him and they all filtered out of the museum. Elizabeth followed and locked the doors behind them, then leaned against it and sighed. The crisis was averted...for now.

Untying her bonnet, she looked around at the exhibits and her workstation. She frowned...for something seemed wrong. Looking more closely, she saw that the *Coelophysis* skull was missing.

Where was it? Who had taken it? Janney? Surely not...one of the other men? Why would they want an unprepped skull of a chicken-sized dinosaur?

She sighed heavily. What to do about it? She had no evidence it had been taken, and to raise a ruckus over it, especially after the near miss of having the museum closed down, seemed misplaced. And yet, the skull was missing.

She bit her lip and made another inspection. A cluster of scales from an Ordovician fish was also gone. It had been small—the size of a large apple. Both things could easily have disappeared into pockets.

First things first. She needed to pay the rent that she suspected had already been paid. The money was not in the bank, but in the cabin.

As she walked back toward her home, she swung her bonnet from its ribbons for a moment, before remembering what she was doing. With a sigh, she pulled it on and tied it as she went along. Upon reaching the cabin she went in, shutting the door securely behind her. After closing the window curtain, she went to her father's room and pulled out the large concordance on the left hand side. Opening it, she flipped through the pages, hunting for dollar bills secreted there.

Only they were gone.

Panic seized her. She knew her father had not taken the money—where had it gone? Then she remembered Daniel had been left alone in the cabin. Had he stolen it? And just as importantly—how was she to pay Janney?

The door opened, and her mother came in. Elizabeth ran from the room and her mother jumped, hand on her chest.

"Oh! Lizzie! When did you get home?"

"Only just now. Ma, what happened to the money in the concordance?"

"It should be there. I saw it a couple of weeks ago."

She shook her head. "There's nothing there now."

Her mother dropped her shawl and sprinted to the room, lifted the tome and flipped wildly through the pages. Sighing, she sat on the bed and stared off.

"It's worse, Ma. The men came into town and found a notice on the museum door saying we needed to get out for nonpayment. Father thought he paid, but isn't sure. I just came back from there. Janney says we can stay, but I have to pay him by Friday."

Her mother stared for a moment, then took a deep breath and said, "I have an idea." She went to the dresser, opened a drawer, and pulled out a small wooden box from inside an old corset. She set the box down on top of the dresser and opened it. Sorting through the miscellaneous items, she finally pulled out what she was looking for, a golden pendant set with a large emerald and small diamonds, and matching earrings.

They had been Elizabeth's grandmother's, and were family heirlooms. But they were valuable, and the only thing they had in the world to barter for the museum. She thought for a moment what would happen to her father if the museum were lost, and she could not bear it. But Grandmother's emeralds...

Her mother looked at her. "It's okay, Lizzie. We can't let them beat us."

Slowly, Elizabeth lifted the necklace and earrings. She stared at them for a moment before placing them in her pocket. Then she headed toward the front door, one slow step at a time.

The town hall appeared full of people when she arrived, and all of them seemed to want to speak to the mayor. She stood off to one side, waiting her turn as person after person disappeared into his office. Finally, it was her turn. Just then, Mrs. Larramendy arrived, her large bust parting people like the prow of a ship parting waves. Her steely glance fell upon Elizabeth.

"Ah. My dear, would you allow me to go before you? This is a matter of great importance. Someone has tried to poison one of my cats!"

Eyes growing wide, Elizabeth said, "Oh no! Of course."

The door to the office opened and a gentleman came out, looking somewhat disgruntled and Mrs. Larramendy went in. Her strident tones echoed through the wooden walls, interspersed with Janney's attempts to speak.

Elizabeth watched the clock tick ever closer to five

o'clock, her hands clenched before her.

Finally, the door opened and Mrs. Larramendy came out. Her chin was up and she sailed away, presumably satisfied as Elizabeth rose and entered the office.

Dark wood paneling lined the walls. A bookcase with beautiful ornaments graced one side of the room, while a low table stood against the other with an ornate mantel clock upon it. Janney himself sat at his desk, looking more than a little perturbed.

"Well, do you have it?"

"Um…no. At least, not in cash. But I do have this…" She pulled out the necklace and earrings and set them on the dark wood of the desk.

Janney at first frowned, then he reached for them and picked them up to study close by the lantern. He was silent for a long moment, then looked up. Elizabeth held her breath, not sure what she wanted to hear him say.

"These are quite valuable. Where did you get them?"

Her mouth dropped open. "They were my grandmother's!"

"I have never seen you wear them."

"I have never had cause too. They are too fine for anything in Matson, and I have never been to Denver."

He rolled them around in his palm for a moment. "I'll accept these in lieu of a few month's rent. But do not be late again."

"No, sir." She pushed up from the chair and breathed out a long breath.

The sun had lowered behind the mountains when she reached the street. With the temperature dropping, she hurried home and began a fire. Her mother had started the bread, so she fried some potatoes to go with it. She made sure the iron latch was set on both doors before sitting down to eat her supper. She had made too much on purpose, so that there would be some for breakfast.

The walls fairly rang with the silence as they picked through their supper. After a while, her mother pushed aside her plate and leaned back.

"I'm sorry, Lizzie. I'm rather dull this evening."

"Oh, Ma, so am I."

"We'll get through this."

She pushed a potato piece around her plate and said, "But Ma, you don't know the worst of it. Daniel…Mr. Bridger was a spy for Howell and Wilke."

Her mother's mouth dropped open. "What? But he was sweet on you…I would swear it."

"He certainly played upon my affections. But it is true. Howell tried to take over the site, and called him out on it. He didn't argue."

Mrs. Ingram was silent for a moment. "Lizzie, I can't help but feel there is more to this story."

"Perhaps, Ma, but whatever the story he has used us ill."

They cleaned up together, and both retired early. As Elizabeth settled into bed that night, she replayed the kisses with Daniel in her mind. Surely there had been something sincere about those.

Hadn't there?

Chapter Ten

The men laughed around the fire, but Daniel sat away from them, staring out into the night. He could hear their ribald jokes, but found nothing amusing. All he could think about was what Elizabeth and her father thought about him.

He had known it was risky to get attached to them, given the depth of his deceit, but he had been unable to help himself. Dr. Ingram was an intelligent academic whose eccentricities simply endeared him, while Elizabeth was…

Everything he'd ever dreamed of and more. Intelligent and brave, yet unafraid of mundane tasks of life. She would have worked alongside him through life and made it worth living. Would have—not any longer. She had been unable to even look at him when he left their camp. She would never forget that betrayal.

Somehow he would make her see the truth…whatever that was now.

He blew out a breath and looked up. The moon had risen in the clear night. With it came a drop in temperature that caused him to reach for his coat and pull it on. He had a job to do, and there was still a ways to go before he would be done. He had no time to feel sorry for himself. When all was done, he would make it right.

"Hey Bridger, thinking about old Ingram's

daughter?"

Fire erupted in Daniel's core, but he kept it under control. "Just glad to be done with it."

"And after all that, what did you find out? Nothing, really."

"I know they aren't in with Marsh or Cope."

"Then they won't last. It's Marsh or Cope, or Wilke in the Front Range."

He said nothing. He hated the war over bones but didn't feel free to express those opinions. Instead, he got up, pulled his plate free from his pack and dished up some of the watery stew from the pot over the fire. It smelled unappetizing and he looked at the cook hired by the camp, a rather greasy youth with a runny nose. He swallowed distastefully and pushed the single piece of meat around on the plate before forcing a bite.

He chewed on the tough meat and swallowed, but it sat like a lump in his stomach. He finished off his plate, glad he'd only taken a single ladleful. At least it gave him an excuse to leave camp to go to the creek and wash out his plate and spoon. Anything to get away from the noise and raucous laughter.

He startled a coyote drinking at the creek and watched as it scampered off. In the distance were the mournful calls of wolves. Somewhere out there were bears, and in the higher elevations were wolverines. Plenty of danger without men.

He shook the water off his plate and turned back toward camp. He still needed to dig out the rocks from under his bedroll. The camp was quieter now with men curling into their blankets to sleep. Feeling about, he dislodged several large stones and moved them out of the way before spreading his blanket down and wrapping himself in the other.

Somehow sleep evaded him, tired as he was. The occasional snore broke the relative silence of the night. One of the men, Ray his name was, muttered in his sleep and groaned. Another, who went by Roger, had a high-pitched whistle as he breathed. All through camp the other ten men, Howell included, fell asleep.

He thought back over his debriefing session with Howell. The man's perfect features had twisted somewhat, shifting his expression and shading his eyes.

"What did you find out? Who's behind them?"

"No one. Ingram works for himself."

"I don't believe it...Marsh or Cope..."

"Forget that. He hates what they are doing. He works for himself, funds himself. That's it."

Howell had looked at him evenly, assessing. Then, "How do we break him, then? Wilke wants that sauropod fossil."

"Wilke's going to be disappointed. Nothing will break him. Or his daughter."

"I've broken my share of women...Nothing new."

Fear and rage suddenly gripped him, and he'd struggled to keep it under control. His face had flamed, he knew, but luckily Howell had glanced away as one of the crewmen came up. By the time he had dealt with that, Daniel had himself under control.

He'd been dismissed then, and had gladly turned away to find a place to work on the site. It looked to be a poorly preserved hadrosaur of some kind. The crew was only half-heartedly working to free the fossil. Their sights were all on the Ingram site.

Of course, thinking about the Ingram site brought Elizabeth to the fore of his mind. He closed his eyes, remembering their kisses, and sleep finally found him.

****

Next morning found him chiseling out a hadrosaur tibia. The lower portion was missing, possibly scavenged or decayed away before it could fossilize properly. It would still add to the collective knowledge, just not as much as a thoroughly intact specimen of a rare species...

His hammer slipped and he hit his knuckle, swearing as he did so. He heard a couple chuckles nearby and looked up to see Howell watching him. He stuck his bleeding knuckle in his mouth and rose to go find a bandage. The first aid kit was a mess, and he took some time to organize it after bandaging his hand. When it was all packed neatly back into the canvas bag, he turned to return to his place by the tibia.

Suddenly, a shout went up and he stopped to squint at the ruckus. Big John stood there, swinging a hammer at a lunging animal. It took a moment for him to realize it was a fox. The animal lunged, growling, and John swung again, missing contact. The creature jumped suddenly and latched onto John's burly forearm. With a decisive swipe of his hammer, he knocked the fox off his arm and to the ground where it lay still in a heap.

"It's got the hydrophoby, John. Quick, wash off the bite."

"You need to cut into the bite marks and suck out the tainted blood..."

"That's for snakebites, peckerhead."

"Ain't nothin,'" John said and strode off toward the creek, presumably to wash off the blood from the wounds.

Meanwhile, someone hastily buried the fox away

from the camp. John returned a few minutes later, still bleeding, and wrapped his forearm in a bandage, tied it off and snapped it free with a yank. Everyone went back to work, but there was a spirit of unease in the camp now. One rabid fox meant there were probably more rabid animals around.

Hands shaking as he struggled to steady the chisel, Daniel thought about the Ingrams. They needed to be warned about the presence of rabies in the region. But how could that be accomplished? They certainly wouldn't listen to anything he had to say.

He wondered if Howell would go. Looking up, he located him standing by the water bucket, listening to something Ray was saying, probably about the fox. Daniel picked up his chisel and walked toward him, waiting back until Ray had finished and moved off.

Howell looked at him. "Well, Bridger?"

"Someone needs to tell the Ingram camp about the fox. There could be more sick animals out there."

"We don't owe them anything."

"It's just plain professional courtesy, man. Nothing more than what they would do for us."

Howell considered. "You may be right. I have to head out to Matson this afternoon. I'll think about swinging by there on the way. Suit you?"

Daniel nodded. "Yes. Thank you." He turned away but felt Howell's gaze upon him as he went.

The tibia was halfway free by the time they finished for the day. Howell had mounted his horse and ridden off in the afternoon. Daniel could only hope he truly would stop by and warn the Ingrams. For now, he had more watery stew to endure.

"Hey John, how bad did that fox get you?" one of

the men asked.

The big man shrugged as he shoveled food into his mouth. "Not bad. I ain't got the hydrophoby if that's what yer askin'."

"It can take a while."

John's empty plate crashed to the ground and he clutched at his throat. Then he uttered a deep growl and lunged for Willie, suddenly breaking into laughter when Willie screamed and scrambled away. "Dumb ass!" John yelled after him before bending to pick up his plate and stride purposefully toward the creek.

Willie crept back, picking up his own plate and scraping the sandy remnants into the fire. Daniel joined John at the creek. He looked over at the big man and wondered if that single bite had been enough. John glanced up suddenly and scowled.

"I ain't sick. You can stop staring at me."

"I know, John. Just thinking about something else."

"Your fuckin' Ingrams? I say we run 'em off and take that place over."

"Sheriff might have something to say about that."

John's hooded eyes stared through him. "You think so, eh? Huh." He grinned suddenly and strode away.

Daniel watched him go. He startled as a bush rattled nearby and spun to see what was there. Nothing showed itself. He hurriedly washed his plate and headed back to camp.

Roger brought out his banjo and played by the campfire until late in the night with Ray leading the singing as they went from one rollicking song to another. Daniel listened with a heavy heart, wondering what Elizabeth was doing.

****

The next day dawned with Howell calling out, "Samms, Bridger, take a mule and head into Matson. We need supplies."

Daniel stood, leaving his tools by his pack and heading off to where the mules were tethered. Roger threw the pack saddle onto the back of a short one and tightened the cinch before attaching the coils of rope to it. He grabbed the list of supplies from Howell and nodded to Daniel before heading out.

Daniel let Roger lead, as he didn't know the way. Roger followed the stream west for about an hour before taking a trail marked by a stone cache that bent slightly north by northwest. After another hour, they reached the edges of Matson.

Warmth spread through him as they entered the main street of town. No one batted an eye toward the pair of dusty prospectors and their mule. They stood in line at the store, waiting their turn, when Daniel said, "You mind if I duck out for a moment? I want to check on something."

Roger shrugged. "Sure, whatever."

Daniel straightened his kerchief and his hat and headed up the covered sidewalk. Four shops down, he came to the museum. Expecting it to be locked, he turned the handle of the door, only to find it click and open at his touch.

Before he knew it, he was standing in the open doorway, and Elizabeth was staring straight at him from the other side of the work table.

"How dare you come here!" she muttered angrily, as though struggling to keep her voice down. "Get the hell out!" She flew at him, hands raised as though to attack.

He caught her wrists and held them securely, but lightly. "I know you hate me now, but listen. It isn't all you think."

"How did I know you'd say something like that? If you think I'm going to believe anything you have to say you're mistaken! Now let me go!"

"I'll let you go if you'll be still. Will you?"

She stopped struggling, though her cheeks were red and her eyes flashed. Tentatively he let her go and stood back. She stayed rooted to the spot, but ready to fly at any moment.

"I can't explain now, and I know I am asking the impossible. But you need to trust me. Please."

She swallowed, but her chin was still up. "I can't."

He nodded, ever so slightly. "I understand. Then just listen to me. We killed a rabid fox, but only after it bit one of our crew. You need to be careful. Rabies is in the area around the sites."

She blanched and mouthed the word. After a moment she swallowed and said, "All right. Anything else?"

He paused, then said softly, "Nothing you'd want to hear."

Another heavy moment passed before she said, "Then you best be on your way."

His mouth opened, but he simply turned and walked away.

Chapter Eleven

Elizabeth watched him go, her heart pounding as her brain struggled to make sense of what had just happened. She ran a hand up one arm to try and steady her shaking. But it was no good, and the hand she then raised to her throat still shook.

She moved heavily toward her work table, sat down with a thud, and leaned her head back. Part of her wanted to run after him and beg him to make her understand. But no, there was nothing to understand. He was an enemy scout who had wormed his way into her heart for the sole purpose of getting information. All in an effort to take her father's fossil site.

Well, it hadn't worked.

She sighed and leaned forward, propping her head in her hand. Her heart still pounded from the short encounter. Her wrists tingled from where he had touched her, and the rest of her longed to be touched as well.

Shaking off the feelings was easier said than done. He had been here… here! And she didn't know how she could bear it. She closed her eyes but could still see him standing there, begging her to trust him.

Well, that was not possible. He had been caught spying and that was all there was to it. Her feelings were unfortunate, but she would get over it. Eventually.

After picking up the instrument, she began

scraping the rock from the bone on the oreodont skull. It was emerging like a cicada from its larval shell, smooth and glossy after its delicate coating of shellac.

She worked for another hour, then dusted off her apron and stretched. She picked up her crocheted shawl, locked the door to the museum, and headed for home. The town lay in shadow now, with the sun well below the edge of the mountains. Elizabeth hurried to light the candles and stoke the fireplace. She felt better as the light lifted the pall of darkness.

After a supper of sourdough bread and cheese, she and her mother knitted quietly beside the fire, her mind still whirling from the afternoon. Only now could she consider the other part of what he had said: they had killed a rabid fox.

Had they gotten word to her father? Surely they would have spread the news… But if they hadn't, she needed to somehow tell her father that they needed to be extra careful. Any mammal could be sick.

"Ma, I need to return to the site tomorrow. I heard about a rabid fox at the other camp, and I need to warn Father."

She yawned, then nodded. "Just come back, won't you?"

"Yes, Ma."

The candle had burned low, reminding her that she would have to make more candles soon. It was one way she could save money. Making tallow candles was smelly, messy work, but much cheaper than store-bought wax candles. A glance at her ma showed her she was thinking much the same thing.

She banked the embers of the fire and carried the remnants of the candle upstairs. Her bed rustled as she laid down after undressing. The night air was dropping in temperature, and she shivered between the cold bedsheets. Sighing, she stared up into the rafters of the cabin. She tried not to think of Daniel, but thoughts found their way into her mind, stealing sleep away.

****

Morning came clear and bright through the little window and Elizabeth yawned heavily as she rose. Her mother was up already, she could hear the fire crackling and her mother stirring something in the skillet. She dressed in her old, green calico and pulled on her worn, scuffed boots.

When her mother saw her, she said, "You aren't going out to the site, are you?"

"I have to, Ma, remember? The Howell camp killed a rabid fox. I need to tell Father to be careful."

"And what about you as you go? Who will keep you safe?"

"I'll have my rock hammer in hand, Ma. I'll come back today."

Though clearly unhappy, her mother nodded and Elizabeth headed out. She pulled the door shut behind her, hefting her pack and twitching her skirt out of the way. She lifted the rock hammer—her only defense against anything or anyone. It was early, the sun barely peeking up over the prairie in the distance and the foothills still swathed in darkness. But she needed to leave early so she could get back before sundown.

Someone needed to warn her father about the danger of rabies, or hydrophobia as it was more commonly known. They had no dog to warn them of anything approaching, and with just the three of them, who was there to keep watch at night for wild animals?

She knew her father would not let her stay, but she needed at least to make sure he knew.

As she walked, she started at every sound, lifting her hammer with every potential threat. A hawk flew overhead, catching thermals and spiraling upward. A cluster of deer moved away from her approach, disappearing into the trees.

She considered Daniel's last words to her. Trust him? But what possible excuse could he offer for what he had done? She could think of none. Nothing changed the fact that he had spied upon them and betrayed their trust. Her steps slowed and she stopped on the trail. Truly, was there no explanation?

A sound caught her and Elizabeth spun around. In the bushes to her right something moved. It took her a minute to make out the camouflaged form of a coyote. Desperately thinking, she cast about for everything she knew about rabid animals. The hydrophobia, the growling and aggression, the simply acting unusual…

Was this coyote acting unusual?

It watched her, and she stared back. After a moment, she raised the hammer and shouted. It flinched, but did not run away. Nervous now, she charged a few steps toward it, waving the hammer and shouting.

The coyote ran off, kicking up gravel behind him and disappeared into the head of a gulley. She paused for a moment to catch her breath before moving on, still keeping a lookout around her for any sign of the coyote's return.

Soon she saw the trail of smoke from the campsite's fire and she turned the corner to find four men working the site. Her father half-rose at her appearance, then rushed toward her.

"You're here! Why? What happened with the museum?"

"I was able to pay the missing rent. It is safe for now. But I need to go back. I'm only here because I wanted to make sure you knew about the rabid fox killed at the Howell site."

"What? First I've heard of it. How do you know?"

She hesitated. "They came into town for supplies and I heard them talking about it."

Her father straightened, hands on hips as he surveyed the area around them. "We'll just have to keep watch, then. Bad business, rabies. I hope no one is attacked."

"One of the men in the other site was bitten."

"It can take weeks to show up. We'll keep a lookout."

She glanced around. "How is the dig going? Who is the new man?"

"Carl. He is taking a break from prospecting for gold and is now digging for dinosaurs. More overburden is gone, but still no skull."

"I have faith it is there."

"Going strictly by reason, it probably isn't. But I still hope…"

"I must get back. I just needed to make sure you knew."

He frowned, worried, and pointed to the hammer. "Glad to see you have a weapon, at least."

"Yes," she said. "I pity any person, or thing, that messes with me." She reached out to grasp his hand and then turned to go.

"Elizabeth…"

She turned, "Yes, Father?"

"You know I'm proud of you, yes?"

She smiled. "Yes, Father."

Warmed by the uncharacteristic show of affection, she looked around as she walked along the familiar path. The late morning sun was obscured occasionally by clouds, which hinted at a stormy afternoon. Her pace quickened.

As she went, she fought the tendency of her mind to wander. She needed to stay aware, in case there was an attack, but thoughts of Daniel would intrude. What was he doing over in that enemy camp? Did he think of her?

Movement startled her and she spun to see what was there. Standing by a tree was a dog. It had a rope around its neck, and its ribs and hips showed. Mindful of the disease loose in the wildlife of the foothills, she froze.

The dog gave a little whine and wagged its tail as it stepped forward, dragging the rope. She noted that it was tight around the dog's neck. Hammer at the ready in case it charged, she knelt and held out a tentative hand to it.

Whining again, the dog wiggled its way toward her, finally dropping on the ground and turning its belly up. She patted it hesitantly, then fingered the rope. With her eyes on the dog's mouth, she worked at the knot around its neck. Soon the rope fell free and she stood quickly.

She walked away, but the dog trotted in her wake, following her. "No, no, shoo. Go home." She waved her hands, but it simply shied back a few paces, then crept back toward her.

Observing the dog, she decided to simply walk on and ignore it. Surely it would wander off eventually?

The sun was well overhead by the time she reached the cabin. Still on her heels, the dog laid in the shade, panting. With a sigh, she got a small pan and filled it with water, then set it down beside the dog which drank enthusiastically. Second-guessing herself, she cut a piece of rind from the ham, and a chunk of bread, and went back outside, setting them down beside the water dish.

He gulped them down, bolting them ravenously, then looking up at her as though to ask if there were more.

"That's all. Go home now. Shoo." She waved her hands, but the dog simply perked its ears up and wagged its tail.

Hoping it would leave of its own accord, she went inside. Feeding a stray dog was not the smartest thing to do when rabies was around.

She ate some of the sourdough from the night before, and a piece of ham, and washed up. Her ma was out, probably helping someone, and the museum called. She changed her dress and smoothed her hair before putting on her bonnet. Looking in the mirror, she sighed. Her dress was years out of fashion as was the bonnet. Both were looking a little worn, and she knew she would need to replace them soon. Perhaps a visit to the haberdashers was called for.

Her mother came in as she reached the bottom step and frowned at her. "You're home! But Elizabeth, is that truly your best dress?"

"Yes, Ma. It is."

She thought for a moment. "You need a new dress.

Stop by the haberdashers and get some fabric and buttons."

"But, Ma…how will we pay for it?"

"Put it on my tab. Your father will just have to sell a skull or something."

"You know he hates that…"

"And I hate seeing my daughter going about looking shabby in an old dress. Get some fabric, Lizzie."

Winkler's Haberdashery was at the far end of the town. A bell tinkled as she opened the door. Bolts of cloth lay behind the long counter which held scissors and thimbles. Threads of various colors and weights were stacked neatly in boxes on another table, and to the left, again behind the counter, lay several different laces.

She instantly saw the fabric she wanted. Slate blue, with tiny green leaves and pink flowers scattered about. An image of a dress filled her mind.

Mrs. Winkler's lined face crinkled as she smiled. "Well, Miss Ingram. Needing a new dress?"

"Yes."

"We have some lovely linens…"

"I'm liking that blue calico there on the shelf. How much is that?"

"Oh this? Nice sturdy cotton. A nickel a yard."

Elizabeth calculated the number of yards needed, and after a brief transaction, she left with a packet of fabric and thread, a needle book, and a card of buttons. Her heart beat wildly after agreeing to the price, especially after the theft of their money and the loss of her grandmother's jewelry, but she had only three dresses, and needed another badly. Perhaps her father could sell another skull in Denver…

Carrying her package, she headed to the museum. It had grown dusty, and she spent some time wiping down all the surfaces with a damp cloth. Part of her was hyper aware in case Daniel returned, but she simply reminded herself that he was out at the Howell site, not here in Matson.

The door opened, and she looked up. A young woman, about Elizabeth's age, stood there in an exquisite moss green linen dress. European lace edged the sleeves and collar, and at her throat and ears…emeralds.

Elizabeth's grandmother's emeralds.

Standing with her mouth open, Elizabeth started and tried to cover her astonishment. "Hello Charlotte, how can I help you?" Mayor Janney's daughter was scanning the room with an interesting mix of boredom and astonishment.

"I had always wondered what this place was about," she said languidly. "What on Earth do you do here?"

"I prepare the fossils for display. Some of them are sold to other museums or collectors." She tried not to stare at the jewels, but Charlotte would draw attention to them by fingering the pendant from time to time.

"I see. Well, I suppose I should invite you to the ice cream social we are having a week from Saturday. I do hope you can come."

It was the first time she had been invited to anything done by Charlotte Janney, and her eyebrows shot upward for a moment. "Oh, certainly. I should like that."

"Excellent. We shall see you then." She turned and

walked out of the museum. With a final wave, she was gone.

An ice cream social. She needed her new dress. Oreodont or dress? She would ever so much prefer to work on the oreodont skull, but the dress was demanding her attention. With a groan, she snatched up the packet of fabric and notions and headed back to the cabin.

When she reached the porch, it was to see the dog lying on the rag rug in front of the door. She paused, for its gaze was on her. It rose and she stepped back, only to see it wag its tail and come wiggling up to her.

She sighed. Like it or not, wise or not, she now had a dog. It was tan with black markings on its face and legs, and the crooked tip of its tail. "Well, you need a name. How about... Fido. Do you like that?"

Fido wagged his tail. She patted his head and went inside. The afternoon sailed by as she and her mother measured and cut out the pieces of her new dress, incorporating the new neckline and sleeves into the pattern. After stopping for supper, they worked on stitching the seams of the skirt. The sun went down and she worried a little about Fido being outside in the cold.

"Ma, I think I have a dog."

"So I noticed."

"It seems rather cold outside."

A pause, then a sigh. "Bring the dog inside. Just make sure it doesn't have any ticks on it."

Elizabeth opened the front door and looked at the dog. He glanced past her to the fireplace, then back up at her and wagged his tail. He gave a little shiver for good measure and she stepped back with a huff.

"Come in, then. Let me scrounge up some food for

you."

Fido followed her as she cut another piece of rind from the hanging ham, and another chunk of bread. She laid these on the ground and put a chipped bowl of water beside it, then sat back down in her chair by the fire.

When the dog had finished bolting food and drink, he stretched out on the hearth rug. Elizabeth gazed at him and felt strangely grateful for the dog's company, realizing that she was, in fact, a little lonely. Perhaps it was why Daniel's deceit had been so devastating. She did not make attachments easily, or lightly. And yet, she had welcomed him into her home and heart, only to have him throw both aside.

She sighed. Fido rose and went to the back door and she opened it for him. "Had enough of domesticity, have you?"

After shutting the door, she climbed up the stairs and stripped down to her shift when a strange sound echoed through the cabin, followed by a low bark. She stepped down the stairs and listened. A scratching sound came from the back door and she lifted the iron latch, opened the door and Fido trotted in. He went straight to the banked fire and laid down.

Returning to the loft, Elizabeth lay down on her bed and let her mind wander back to those times Daniel had held her and kissed her. She squirmed a little, thinking that he had not meant any of it, but that didn't mean she hadn't enjoyed it at the time.

She sighed, and gave herself up to memory.

Chapter Twelve

Sparks flew up from the fire, rising to rival the stars before winking out of sight. Daniel watched them, heart and limbs heavy. The men were laughing and joking, shoving one another good naturedly, but they avoided him.

He was fine with that. The only person he needed to get close to was Rufus Howell, and for some reason that man had taken a liking to him. Just the other day he had praised his work, and left him in charge of the whole hind end of the hadrosaur. But to do his job, he needed to get close to Howell, and it wasn't happening fast enough.

With a grunt and an explosion of breath, Rufus Howell sank down on the log next to him. He raised his mug of beer and waited for Daniel to touch it with his own. He took a long draught, licked his lips, and said, "How are you settling in?"

Daniel shrugged and took a sip of his own beer. "Fine, I guess. Fossil work suits me."

"You ever work with any of the big boys? Cope or Marsh or..."

Daniel shook his head. "No. Just little outfits so far for me."

"Who?"

He shrugged again. "No one you would know."

"Try me." Howell's voice had a hard edge to it.

Daniel leaned back. "Let's see, Smith and Reeves, and Gesseldorf. Someone else in there, but I can't remember their name."

"I've heard of Smith and Reeves, but not the other. What did Gesseldorf work on?"

"They found that juvenile *Brontosaurus* up in Wyoming."

"Oh yeah, I heard something about that. Why'd you leave?"

"Got in on the last main season at the site. They transported everything to a museum back east."

Howell was silent for a moment, then said, "I may need your help with the Ingrams again."

Daniel twisted to look at him. "What? No, they won't have anything to do with me now."

"Don't be too sure. You never know…" He pushed up from the log and slipped away, leaving Daniel thinking.

Howell's place was taken by Roger, who sat heavily after refilling his mug yet again from the keg. He belched loudly, his rancid breath mixing with half-digested watery stew and beer. Daniel winced and tried not to breathe.

Roger clapped him on the back and said loudly, "I wish I had your luck! Out here in the middle of nowhere, nothing to give a man a bit of comfort, if you know what I mean."

Daniel shook his head. "Not sure I do."

"Piece of ass and tits. Like that girl you had at the other site. Nice bit of work she was. Did she scream, or was she more of a moaner?"

Daniel shoved him off the log, grabbed him by the open collar, and struck his jaw with his fist. Roger shook it off and lunged to his feet. Daniel ducked and came back up swinging. His other fist connected, knocking Roger backward onto the fire. Tripod, kettle, and cinders flew as he screamed and scrambled free. Roaring now, he came for Daniel who dropped at the last minute to vault Roger over his shoulder and onto his back on the ground.

Daniel spun, fists at the ready, but Roger lay still, struggling to breathe. He gasped several times then rolled onto his stomach to push himself up from the dirt. Daniel rose warily, ready.

With a hand on his chest, Roger gave an ugly look to Daniel. But he shook his head and said, "No more. For now."

Daniel extended his hand but the other ignored it and moved away. Blowing out a breath of relief, he sat back down beside the fire as the other men slowly returned to their business.

Movement to his right caused Daniel to start up, but it was only Howell, who lowered himself onto the log and sat looking at him. Daniel endured it for a few minutes before saying, "Yes? I'm sorry about that."

"Are you, though?"

Daniel shrugged. "He had no business talking about a woman like that."

"Especially that particular woman?"

Daniel considered him. "I'm a professional. I resent anyone insinuating that I would be anything else on a dig site."

After a moment, Howell nodded. "Yes, I can see that. Roger was out of line. He's been begging for a beating a while now."

"Well, he got one." Daniel cracked his neck and

blew out a breath.

"What are your plans?"

"Not sure I know what you mean."

"What are you going to do when the season is over?"

Daniel shrugged. "Might head out to California. Take the train and see what happens."

"You aren't going back east to one of the museums to help prep the bones?"

"I don't know if this is what I'll do for the rest of my life." Daniel hoped it sounded convincing.

"Where's home?"

"If you mean where did I come from, then Philadelphia. Don't really have a home."

Howell nodded. "Well, you got the skills to go far with paleontology if you choose. I could probably get you on with Stanthorpe."

Daniel schooled his face to look interested. "Yeah? That could be interesting. How do I do that?"

"Just keep doing what you're doing. I'll speak to him about it." He stood and stretched. "Time to turn in. See you in the morning."

Daniel sat staring at the fire for a few minutes longer. Now that he was calmer, he saw the folly in allowing Roger to provoke him like that. He had declared himself to these men, and he didn't know any of them. He had known Elizabeth was a problem for him, he just hadn't known how much of one.

He would have to be on his guard. He could not afford to bring this much attention on himself. The fact that it had, in a strange turn of events, strengthened Howell's opinion of him was just a serendipitous event. It could so easily have gone wrong…

****

It was a week later when he was called to take a volunteer and a mule into town to pick up supplies. His heart jumped at the thought of perhaps seeing Elizabeth. While Eddie saddled the mule, he got the list from Howell, who went over a few things before adding. "You'll need to stay overnight. Got something coming on the train and it doesn't come into town until late. Get a cart from Riggs. You'll need it."

Daniel nodded, and headed back. He passed John, who rubbed and flexed his arm. He had removed the bandage to expose the puncture wounds from the fox's bite.

Daniel frowned, "What's wrong?"

"Arm just feels strange, kinda jangly."

"Jangly?"

"Yeah, like bells going off or something." Big John shook himself and lifted a sledgehammer before heading off.

Daniel watched him go, then walked slowly over to where Eddie stood waiting with the mule. He checked the ropes before motioning to the other to head on out.

Matson was booming when they arrived. A wagon train had made its way into town and there were people everywhere. He went to the hotel first, only to find it booked. As a second choice, he walked to Mrs. Goode's and secured a single room they would have to share. Daniel didn't care; he would be on an actual bed that night.

After dropping off his list of supplies with Hutchins and securing a cart, he parted ways with Roger who headed for the only brothel in town. Daniel stepped up onto the wooden sidewalk and down two storefronts from the end. The museum was open, and there were people inside. He saw Elizabeth in a new dress, her hair braided and secured at the back of her head. He watched her, unobserved, for a moment as she talked knowledgeably with a woman.

She caught sight of him and frowned. The woman moved away and Elizabeth turned to him with a forbidding expression. "What are you doing here?"

"I thought it was open to the public."

"You know what I mean. I should think you'd be done with us."

He dropped his voice. "I'll never be done with you."

Her eyes flickered, and she swallowed, but made no reply.

He straightened and said, "I'll leave you to your guests. I'll come back."

With a final long look at her, he left, striding purposefully along to the general store where the cart was being loaded. He reminded them to leave the back of it clear for the train cargo and went to the hotel to get something to eat that wasn't watery stew or soup.

As he cut into his steak and savored the first bite, the chair next to him scraped along the floor and Stanthorpe Wilke sat. Daniel set his fork down.

Wilke's hand came up. "No, no, don't let me interrupt your meal. It must be a nice change from camp food."

"Yes, sir. It is." He allowed himself a smile which Wilke returned.

"I've been hearing good things about you."

"From where?"

"Just around. You're apparently quite talented with

preparation work."

Daniel took another bite of his steak. "I like it, at any rate."

"I don't know if you are aware, but I have a crew that stays on over the winter to prep the specimens we get in summer."

"So I'd heard."

"I'm offering you a spot on the team."

Daniel made his eyebrows rise and his mouth drop open. "Does it pay?"

"Half again as much as crew work, plus a bonus when you're done."

He nodded, gaze on Wilke. "Do I have to answer now?"

Wilke lifted his hands. "No, no. Take all the time you need. I understand."

"Okay, I will. Very seriously."

Wilke slapped the table. "You do that. I'll be heading out—driver is waiting for me."

Daniel watched him go and meditatively finished his steak.

The train was due around seven, which meant they'd need to be there by six just in case it arrived early. He looked at the mantel clock over the fireplace. It was nearly six now. He got up, paid for his meal, and headed out toward the train station.

He saw Roger waiting by the station. He grinned when he saw Daniel.

"I didn't see you at Miss Kate's."

"I wasn't there. Had a couple errands to do, and got some supper at the hotel."

"I'm broke, but it was worth it!"

From the distance a whistle sounded and they

stopped talking to strain to see the train. Smoke appeared, then the train puffed into the station. It came to a screeching halt and people began disembarking and getting on. Daniel went to stand by a box car that was being unloaded.

"I'm here for some cargo for Rufus Howell?"

The workers disappeared into the car, then appeared holding a box between them. They set it down carefully and looked at him.

"You planning on blowing up the bank?"

He laughed, leaving Daniel confused until he looked at the crate. He saw one word—nitroglycerine.

Dynamite? What did Howell need with dynamite? Surely not to blast through the overburden and risk damaging the fossils? Between them, he and Eddie carried the crate to Hutchins and placed it on the cart. Then they turned toward the edge of town, and Mrs. Goode's.

****

The next morning, after a bowl of lumpy gruel, Daniel wiped his mouth and said to Eddie. "Gonna run and do a couple of things. I'll meet you at Hutchins's."

"Sure, sure."

Roger helped himself to another bowl and settled back in at the table. Daniel tied his kerchief around his neck and headed out.

Something was laying on the rag rug in front of Elizabeth's door. As he approached, it got to its feet and growled. When he was close, it barked until the door opened.

Elizabeth stood there in her old, faded dress with her hair tumbled all around her. She'd obviously been interrupted in the process of doing her hair. Daniel had to catch his breath at the sight of her like this. It felt intimate, and he wanted to pull her to him and kiss her hard.

He didn't. Instead, he pointed to the dog. "What is that?"

"It's a dog."

"I know that, but why do you have a dog when rabies is going around? Don't you know—"

"Yes, I know. But he doesn't have it and he just came along. Here, Fido. Come."

The dog slunk back toward her and she looked up at him, anger in her eyes. Concern for her made him sound harsher than he intended, but still! She had to see how ill-advised it was to take in a stray dog with rabies running rampant through the mammal population.

"You need to get rid of that dog. I'll do it for you if you want."

"You'll do nothing of the sort. The dog stays. I can make my own decisions about such things."

"Clearly you can't! You've taken on a stray that you know nothing about!"

"I know that he is a sweet dog, and good company, and will keep me safe when I have to walk out to the site, as I am doing today."

"You shouldn't be walking about alone."

"It is none of your concern what I do. I am an adult, and nothing to do with you. I will make such decisions myself."

He seethed. Worry exaggerated his feelings and he slammed his hand against the door post. The dog barked at him, and Elizabeth flicked back a long swath of hair and looked ready to attack him as well. He stepped back, holding up his hands in defeat.

"I'm sorry. I overstepped my bounds. But please be careful, Miss Ingram. Despite all appearances, I care deeply for your safety."

Her expression softened, and her eyes sparkled with unshed tears. She hastily bent, pulled the dog into the house, and shut the door.

Head bowed, he turned slowly toward town.

Chapter Thirteen

Elizabeth leaned against the door, knowing Daniel was on the other side. Her eyes smarted with unshed tears, and she breathed out harshly, angry with herself for being so weak before him. After a moment, she climbed back up the stairs to finish securing her hair.

When she was done, she made her way to Riggs's to rent a mule. Her father had asked her to bring supplies to the camp on Thursdays, and so she hoped to get back before sunset to return the mule and sleep in her own bed that night.

Fido trotted at her heels, true to his name. He growled at the mule at first, but settled down as she led it along to the general store. She secured it to the post out back, then went in and gave her list to Mr. Hutchins, explaining about the mule. He simply nodded and told her they would take care of it. She turned in time to see Daniel watching her from across the store.

She pretended to look at the men's hats. A shadow crossed her and she glanced up to see Daniel standing beside her.

"Does your father need a new hat?"

"Why are you speaking to me? Surely you have other, more important, things to do."

"Nothing as important as this."

She closed her eyes. "Leave me alone, Mr. Bridger."

He bent down so his lips buzzed her ear when he spoke. "I can't leave you alone, Elizabeth."

She turned to look up at him, but he was already gone. Just then she was called that her order was ready, so she shook herself and went out the back to take control of the mule.

Fido was nowhere to be seen, so she headed off, hoping he would be all right, wherever he was. However, after fifteen minutes she heard a bark and looked down to see him racing toward her. He stood beside her as she stopped, wagging his tail and panting from the exertion. She tousled his ears and set off again.

The dig site was busy when she arrived, with easily seven men total working on the *Camarasaurus*. Her father caught sight of her and beamed, straightening immediately and coming toward her.

"Elizabeth! You're here! Is it Thursday already?"

She chuckled, slightly out of breath. "Yes, Father. I've brought the supplies. I hope it is enough. I see you have more helpers."

"Yes, more men down on their luck, but good workers the lot of them. I'm sure Charlie will make the supplies last."

"Charlie?"

"Yes, he has proven to be quite the talented camp cook."

"Well, that is excellent. But I must be getting back. I see they have stripped the mule bare of the supplies."

His hand on her shoulder tightened momentarily. Suddenly, his attention was drawn by Fido. "Who is this fellow?"

"Ah, Fido. He found me when I was on my way home last time."

"So you have a dog, now."

"So it would seem. He is good company."

"I am glad to see it, then. Just be careful, rabies."

"I will."

She kissed him, then took hold of the mule's lead rope and started back down the trail. Fido trotted at her heels while the mule plodded along beside her. She kept an anxious eye on the sky, for the sun sank ever lower in the sky.

The first stars peeked out of a twilight sky by the time she handed the mule back to its owner and turned her tired steps toward home. Fido panted, though his ears were still up. Still, he flopped down on the hearth rug after drinking from his water dish and stretched out.

It was late, and she was hungry. A little bit of bread remained, and some stew from the night before, but she gave those to the dog and made some cornbread instead. She slathered it with butter and drizzled honey over it, then cut a sliver of cheese to go with it.

A knock came at the door and she rose to answer it. Mrs. Heggedy stood there, stooped and wizened from years on the edge of the prairie. She held a basket covered with an embroidered towel. She grinned, and lifted the towel to uncover seven chicks huddled together. With the towel off, they began to peep, charming Elizabeth immediately.

"They're ready, a week old today, and I told everyone you asked first for some of the babies. Here they are."

Elizabeth took the basket, gently touching the little bodies. Fido had come up, interested, and she hesitantly scooped one up and lowered it in her hand to his nose. He sniffed, and his tail wagged.

"That will be good. Raise them from babies with the dog and he'll likely leave them alone."

"Well, I hope so. Thank you, Mrs. Heggedy."

She closed the door and took the basket with its peeping crew into the kitchen. Fido followed, nosing into the peeping, fuzzy mass and snorting when he got a noseful of fluff. She found a crate outside and brought it in, laying an old towel in the bottom and putting a small dish of water inside. The chicks ran around, peeping wildly, greatly exciting Fido. She found another towel and draped it over the crate, and soon the peeping died down as the chicks went to sleep.

"I'm tired, too, Fido. Can I trust you here with them?"

In answer, he lay down on the hearth rug again and she stood slowly, then headed up the stairs to bed.

****

She woke to excited barking early the next morning. Running down the stairs, she was met with a flurry of fuzzy bodies and Fido apparently attempting to herd them together. Her mother scampered after the chicks. Elizabeth scurried about for several minutes, scooping the chicks up and replacing them in the crate. She found a board, and after spreading some of the seed out for them in the bottom of the crate, covered the chicks up.

"Whew. I guess I will need to find a way to contain these little things."

"How are we going to feed them?"

"Mrs. Heggedy gave me a small bag of feed. I'll go to Rigg's and get more later. For now, we need to contain them."

After sharing the last of the cornbread with Fido

and cutting him a bit of meat from the roast she had bought, she went outside to look around. The remains of a large packing crate stood next to the back wall of the cabin. Some large fossil had been transported in it. With a few modifications, it was soon habitable for the chicks. She removed some of the boards from the top, hoping they would still be unable to get out, but wanting them to have some natural light. Then she placed the smaller crate inside with a pan of water and another pan of food. Hopefully they would stay safe...

Next on the list was a bath. The day after was the social at Charlotte Janney's home. Her new dress was clean and pressed, and she had blacked her good boots to the best of her ability. They were now presentable...ish. Nothing she had would compare with Charlotte, but at least she would not look too out of line.

Except Charlotte now had her grandmother's necklace and earrings.

She tried not to think about that as her mother helped her drag the tub out and begin heating water. She needed to wash her hair as well, and always hated that. The cold, clinging strands of her long hair gave her the shivers. But, it needed to be done. As she washed and rinsed the thigh-length hair, she wondered what it would be like to have short hair, like men. Laughing aloud, she finished rinsing her hair and dried it in a towel.

After twisting it up onto the crown of her head, she proceeded to bathe herself. The water had grown cool, and she hurried to finish her bath before it grew even cooler. Finally, she was wrapped in her mother's old dressing gown and sitting in front of the fire.

It took a long time for her hair to dry, and then she had to brush it out and plait it. Her mother had the little chunk of meat simmering with an onion and broth over the fire and another sourdough loaf in the Dutch oven. The next day was the social; the following day was Sunday. Then Monday with its laundry and heavy work.

She closed her eyes and once again Daniel's voice whispered in her ear. The twisting pain in her chest started again. Why had he betrayed them? And why did she still want to believe him?

Fido scratched at the back door and she went to let him in. In his mouth was a rabbit, and she shooed him back outside after praising his prowess. At least she wouldn't need to feed him that night.

Her mother lifted her shawl off the peg and wrapped it around her shoulders. "Lizzie, I need to go out. Mrs. Devlin is having her baby, and someone needs to look after the other children."

"All right, Ma. I'll see you later."

"Don't wait up."

Elizabeth went out back to check on the chicks. They were scratching and peeping at the bottom of the box. She was concerned that some snake or weasel would find a way in and kill her babies, but she had no other option for housing them, unless she brought them inside at night. Which, after a moment's thought, she decided to do.

By the time the sun was setting over the mountains, the chicks had clustered together in the smaller crate and she picked it up and carried it inside, them put a board over the top with a few books over that to hold it down. Fido still munched away on his rabbit, some distance beyond the back door, so she locked it when she got inside. But, she kept an ear open for his scratching when he was ready.

Supper was ready, and she lifted the lid with its coals off the Dutch oven. Using a long-handled fork, she pulled the loaf out and set it on a plate, then on the table. The meat had fallen apart and she thickened the gravy before ladling some onto her plate and cutting a slice of hot bread from the loaf. She added plenty of butter and set it on her plate until the butter had melted.

As she ate, she read the latest journal on paleontology and western life. Someone had found a nest of eggs in Montana, and she read with interest about them. She sighed at the thought of making so momentous a find.

Darkness had enveloped the town, and she heard a scratching at the back door. After rising to let Fido in, she checked on the chicks who were clustered together with their eyes closed. Fido stood at the back door with the hind leg of the rabbit. Elizabeth and he stared at each other for a full minute as she considered whether or not to let him in. Finally, she sighed and opened the door wider to admit him. He went straight to the hearth rug and laid down, rabbit leg between his paws.

The candle had burned low by the time she locked the doors and carried it upstairs to her loft. The cold evening air had settled up there, causing her to shiver a little as she untied the dressing gown and slipped between the covers of her bed. She could not help but think of Daniel as she lay in the darkness, wondering if he were thinking of her…

****

A low bark woke her the following morning and

she realized she had slept in. The sun was high above the horizon as she swung her legs clear of the bed and pulled the dressing gown on around her. The stairs felt smooth and cold to her feet as she trotted down. Fido paced by the back door, the bones of the rabbit's hind leg still scattered before the fire.

Elizabeth let him out, then picked up the bones to toss outside. She dropped them into the chicken coop at the last minute before loosing the chicks into it. They ran about peeping and she grinned as she watched them. After scattering some feed around them, she went back into the house.

The social was set for one, and included a light luncheon before the ice cream. It had been years since she'd had any, and she looked forward to experiencing it again.

Her hair. She needed to do something with her hair. Her fingers danced as they unbraided it. With long, smooth strokes she brushed it out, then secured it high on the back of her head before braiding it. Once it was plaited into a smooth rope, Elizabeth coiled it up into a bun that took up the whole back of her head, finishing it off with a pair of combs her mother had given her and curling the tendrils that hung about her face with the curling iron.

Looking this way and that in the mirror, she slipped some earrings on and then pulled on the new dress. The slate blue made her cheeks and lips seem pinker and she bit her lips to make them redden.

She wore all her petticoats to give form to the skirt and wished for her grandmother's emeralds. But Charlotte Janney had those, and she had to try and get used to the fact.

After lacing up her boots, she stood back to see herself in the dressing table mirror. While not the height of fashion, she looked well enough to attend a higher society function. Her chest rose as she breathed deeply, hoping for a little more courage.

Her mother sighed as she came down the stairs. "Ah, Lizzie, you do look fine!"

"Thank you, Ma. I am rather nervous."

"Nonsense. Just sit and listen and enjoy the food."

"I don't really fit in…"

"You're a young lady of Matson, that's enough."

She shut the door behind her, leaving Fido inside and stepped off the porch to head across the way and down the main street. The Janneys lived in a large house on a side street near the middle of town. She walked sedately, nodding to people she passed and noting the surprise in their eyes. It irritated her somewhat. *I don't usually look that bad…do I?*

Her boots clattered against the wooded slats of the sidewalk until she reached Gordon Street and the sidewalk ended. She stepped hesitantly down onto the dirt, imagining a mass of dust accumulating on her shoes and skirt by the time she reached the Janneys.

Across the way she saw Mary Liesle, obviously intent upon the Janney house as well. She smiled a greeting and said, "Ah! Mary, I take it you are going to Charlotte's social as well."

Mary nodded, as though too nervous to speak. But she took Elizabeth's proffered elbow and sighed. "Indeed yes. I'm afraid there will be ever so many people there."

"No doubt. But friends, all." Still, her own heart beat faster the closer they came to the front door.

Elizabeth leaned forward and pulled the bell, then stood back waiting.

James, Charlotte's younger brother, opened the door. He motioned them into the parlor where Charlotte stood with several other young women, including Lydia Hutchins who smiled and lifted a hand. Her head tilted backward as she laughed at something someone had said.

"Ah, Mary, Elizabeth! Welcome. Well! We're all here."

Just then a portly form with elaborate hair appeared. Mrs. Janney said, "Charlotte, the luncheon is ready. You can bring your guests through."

Elizabeth tried not to stare, but the house was full of wallpaper and wainscot. Shelves and bric-a-brac were everywhere, creating a fantastic setting for the immaculately dressed Charlotte. Elizabeth struggled under the conviction that her dress was much inferior to those around her.

Instantly, her chin came up a notch. She would not let anyone coerce her into thinking she was less than anyone... much less herself. All of the girls had done their best with what they had, and rather than criticize them to make herself feel better, she tried instead to admire each and every one. They were an isolated cluster of young women in the American West. All of them had done wonders with limited means.

Ingrid, the parson's daughter, looked down her long nose at Elizabeth. "I don't see you on Sundays at church."

"Er, no. My parents were never much for it, and I'm afraid I have never gotten in the habit."

"You miss out on so many wholesome activities. It

would give you such relief from the constant grind with your father's work."

"I like my father's work, though. My problem is that I don't have enough time to devote to it. So many things like laundry and cooking get in the way."

"But those things come first, as they should."

Elizabeth twisted inside, wishing she had been seated beside someone else. "You should come to the museum sometime and see what we have. You would see what I mean."

Ingrid's head tilted lightly to one side. "Perhaps I will. I pass by it all the time and wonder what goes on there."

"Well, it is a dusty endeavor, as you will see."

They were distracted by the serving of a platter of tiny sandwiches cut into a variety of shapes and filled with different meats. Little plates filled with salads of fruits such as strawberries and a whole orange with the peel cut and shaped like that of a flower were set before each girl. Charlotte looked on with pride.

Most of the girls were hesitant to eat, but Charlotte led the way. A younger brother sneaked in and reached toward the sandwiches, only to have Charlotte slap his hand away, sending him crying into the next room. His voice rose to high levels and soon Mrs. Janney appeared with him still howling until given the coveted sandwich.

"Mother, please remove him."

"Come, Davey, we'll go read your books."

Once Charlotte had finished her fruit and sandwiches, she rose and led the girls back to the parlor where a large spinet sat. The girls took turns playing or singing, at differing levels of accomplishment. When it came time for Elizabeth, she simply shook her head.

"I'm afraid my time has been spent preparing fossils instead. I have nothing with which to entertain you."

Charlotte smiled condescendingly and looked up as a small cart with exquisite china dishes and little silver spoons was brought down the hall to the parlor. She stood and made a great show of serving each girl from one of the dishes in which a large scoop of ice cream lay.

It was as good as Elizabeth remembered, and she savored every spoonful. As soon as she put down her spoon, the bell rang and Charlotte's older brother shot to the door to open it. Elizabeth had stood to go place her bowl on the cart near the hallway, when she came face to face with Daniel.

Shock registered on his face as they both stood stock-still.

Mr. Janney came down the stairs and said, "Ah, Daniel. Come into my office and tell me what is going on at the dig." Daniel shot her a somewhat frightened look and followed the mayor off to the other side of the house.

"I didn't know you were acquainted with Mr. Bridger, Elizabeth. But then, he does similar work to your father," Charlotte said.

"Yes, we have met."

Turning to the other girls, Charlotte said, "He is a young paleontologist working for my father. He's practically in charge of the whole site. He reports every week to Father, who is financing part of the expedition along with Mr. Wilke, the Denver millionaire."

Elizabeth tried not to look anywhere, or at anyone.

The girls talked amongst themselves. She tried to focus on what they were saying, but it was no good. She stood, and the room went quiet as she struggled for a voice.

"I'm sorry, Charlotte, but I must go. I left my dog in the house and he must need to get out by now."

"I didn't know you had a dog."

"It followed me home from the dig site a few days ago."

Elizabeth had barely shut the door behind her when laughter broke out from the direction of the parlor. She held her head up as she walked away. It was a relief to be away from the others.

But what was Daniel doing at the Janney house? Why had he been meeting with the mayor?

Chapter Fourteen

Mayor Janney liked the sound of his own voice, he decided. The man talked incessantly, and Daniel was trying desperately to get away. And yet, the mayor droned on…

"And so I said to Stanthorpe—that's Stanthorpe Wilke, of course—Stanthorpe, you need to expand your collection. You need to go for a *Tyrannosaurus* now, get something really big in the minds of the public. Think what you could make on something like that. Not this measly hadrosaur."

"The problem is finding a *Tyrannosaurus*," he interjected.

The mayor brushed away such impracticalities. "Get the right intelligence, apply the right pressure, and you have your fossil site."

"Excuse me, Mayor, but I need to get on the trail if I am going to get back by nightfall."

"Oh right, of course! Yes, yes, on your way. Don't forget what I said to tell Rufus now."

"No, sir, I won't. Thank you." He shook the proffered hand and practically ran down the stairs to peer into the parlor. He ignored Charlotte's attempts to engage him and left, shutting the door behind him.

He had to get to her. *God knows what she must think of me.* And yet, what could he tell her? Nothing. Nothing of substance anyway. His feet slowed and he stopped, thinking. After all, what good would it do to see Elizabeth now?

He started walking again. Good or not, right or wrong, he was going to see her and try to find a way to make it right.

As soon as he stepped on her porch, a loud barking set up from inside the house. He paused for a moment, hearing a voice hush the dog as someone came toward the door. He knocked, and the barking intensified, even as the door opened.

Without giving her the option to speak, he slipped inside, letting the growling dog pin him against the wall. Elizabeth closed the door and turned to him, hands on hips.

"What are you doing here?"

"Just…" What was he going to say?

She looked ethereal in the semidarkness of the cabin. The sun had gone behind the mountains and she had only the fire and a couple of candles to light the interior. He held up his hands.

"Can you calm the dog?"

She bent and stroked the head of the agitated beast. Its barks slowed, then stopped, though a steady growl persisted. Then she looked up, and his heart leapt when her gaze locked on his.

"There, he is calm. Please say what you need to say and go."

His voice caught in his throat as he tried to think of what to say. "I…I know how it looks."

"It looks like you are in the pay of Janney and Wilke. But I knew that."

"I'm not…it isn't…you don't understand."

"Please don't treat me like some imbecile, Mr.

Bridger. I am perfectly capable of understanding that your priorities lie with a group of men who use underhanded tactics against others."

He stared at her, slowly shaking his head. "It simply isn't what you think."

Her gaze did not soften. "I need you to go now, Mr. Bridger."

"Miss Ingram… Elizabeth… I need you to say you trust me."

Slowly he reached for her, and she did not resist when he grasped her hand. He drew her closer, even though the growling intensified. Then she was in his arms, and he bent to kiss her.

His lips brushed hers, then he pulled back and whispered, "Say you'll trust me."

"I can't." She pulled away and turned from him. "Please go."

With a feeling of helplessness, he released her and opened the door. "I'm not letting you go, Elizabeth."

She said nothing and he closed the door. Frustrated, he glanced at the darkening sky and decided to stay in town one more day rather than try to walk back to the site in the dark.

The hotel was quiet for once, and he sat at an unoccupied table to have some supper before going up to his room. There was someone sitting at the bar who looked somewhat familiar. He kept peering round at Daniel, giving him an uncomfortable feeling. He looked up, only to see the figure was gone. After a minute of focus on his elk steak, movement caught his eye as a shadow appeared suddenly and sat.

Dark shock of greasy hair and sparse beard, Freddie MacMillan stared at him. He had been kicked off the crew a week before and looked the worse for wear.

"Freddie. You're looking rough."

"Been living rough for a while. Saw you at the Ingrams'."

His mouth started to drop open, but he controlled it. "Just checking on an old friend."

"Not really in Janney's interests, though, is it?"

"Don't know what you mean. We're all colleagues of a sort."

Freddie smiled a little. "I'm willing to bet neither Janney nor Rufus knows you went to see the Ingram girl."

Cold touched Daniel's heart, then traced a trail down his back. "Don't know that it's anyone's business."

"Janney's paying your way. It's his business all right." He chuckled at Daniel's discomfort and added, "Look, I ain't gonna tell. Don't care one way or another. How about you buy me a nice dinner and a drink or two, and we'll call it even?"

Daniel nodded. "Okay, I can do that... for an old crewmate, after all."

"Yeah, yeah. That's right." He waved the host over and ordered a large steak and bourbon, then sat back with a satisfied expression. When his drink came he gulped it down and ordered another.

Daniel was forced to watch him chew his steak with an open mouth and slurp bourbon. Finally, drunk and nearly incoherent, Freddie tottered to his feet and with a smile and a salute, headed out of the hotel.

Daniel rose and went heavily up the stairs to his room. After stripping down, he climbed into bed and lay, staring up at the ceiling for a long time. When sleep did come, it was fitful and uneasy.

He woke late, startled by the height of the sun and jumping up to dress and pack. Smoothing his hair, he went downstairs to eat and settle up his bill before leaving. The sheriff stood talking to the maître d, who pointed to him and said, "He bought the man his meal last night."

Daniel frowned. "What?"

"The vagrant known as Freddie MacMillan. He was found dead outside the house of Mayor Janney. Looks like he fell and hit his head… Maybe something else. What did you talk about last night?"

Daniel shrugged. "Nothing in particular. Discussed the dig we're both working at under Rufus Howell for the mayor, but nothing else."

"He wasn't threatening you or anyone else?"

Daniel shook his head. "No. Not that I recall."

The sheriff levied an even look at him. A minute went by. "Well, if you think of anything, let me know."

"Sure will. Right now I gotta head back to the dig." He shouldered his pack and headed out.

Dead? MacMillan dead? How had it happened? Had he really fallen, or had someone struck him down? Who could have killed the man, and did anyone know he had a motive for the murder?

His pace quickened as he crossed Main Street and went past the general store to the trailhead. Keeping an eye out for attacking animals, he made his way back to camp unimpeded.

He set his pack down in his spot and put his oiled canvas jacket over it. The sky was gray and turbulent, and it looked to be an uncomfortable afternoon. Howell had finally gotten a couple tents set up for the men to sleep in on stormy nights, but it was close quarters and the smells from so many unwashed bodies could be overwhelming.

He noted Big John still rolled up in his blankets and turned a questioning face toward Howell, who motioned him over. Speaking low, he said, "John ain't well today. Complaining of aches and things. Should we be concerned?"

Daniel looked over to where John shook under his blanket, muttering. He nodded slightly, and looked Howell in the eye. "We'll need to watch him."

Howell breathed out a frustrated breath and ran a hand over his head. "Damn it. This will spook the crew."

"We'll just watch him for now. May be ague."

"Yeah, could be."

Just then one of the men came up. "Hey boss, I just tried to give John some water and he wouldn't take it. Said he couldn't. He's sick, ain't he?"

"Yeah, he's pretty sick. We'll all just have to look after him."

"It ain't the hydrophoby, is it?"

"Well, was he afraid of the water you tried to give him?"

"Naw, just said no and turned away."

"Okay, then, there you go. Get back to work."

Howell and Daniel exchanged a look. Just then a raindrop fell. The sky thickened and lighting began to flicker in the distance, thunder rolling long moments after. Men leaned their tools up against a boulder and ran for the shelter of the tents. Howell lit a lantern and Daniel sat. One by one, the rest of the men in the tent joined him.

Outside, the storm ramped up, winds beginning to blow and sweep debris along in the thick raindrops hitting the ground. The intensity of the drops increased, when suddenly, there was a roar from outside.

Daniel shouted, "John! We've left him."

But the flap to the tent ripped aside and John's half-naked body was lit from behind by a crash of lightning. The man stumbled to one side and slowly righted himself before roaring some unintelligible words at them. Daniel surged to his feet, only to hear Rufus shout, "Get down, Bridger!"

He ducked, and a shot rang out, rivaling the thunder outside. John's roar paused, then gurgled, and he fell backward out of the tent. Silence reigned, save for the storm outside.

Daniel turned to see Howell standing with his revolver in his hand, a little stream of smoke snaking from the barrel. He caught Howell's look. and said, "You shot him?"

"You saw him. Sick with rabies I'll wager. What could I do?" His voice faded as Daniel ran outside and knelt beside John, who was coughing up blood. After a couple minutes, with water streaming down over them, the coughing stopped and John relaxed into the spattering mud. Daniel looked up through the pouring rain at Howell.

"What do we do now?"

"We'll have to bury him."

"We need to take him into Matson. Talk to the sheriff."

"How? No one's gonna touch him to get him onto a mule."

"We have to let Doc Pirie look at him."

"Can't do anything until this storm ends. C'mon, let's get back inside."

Daniel bent to pick up one of John's legs to drag him into the tent but Howell shoved him.

"Leave him, get inside."

Stumbling into the tent, Daniel accepted the blanket one of the men handed him and dried off. Outside, the storm lessened somewhat, and soon blew over, leaving just a sprinkling of rain behind. Daniel clomped through the mud to where the mules were tethered and undid the shortest mule, leading it back to where John lay glassy-eyed.

He called a couple of men over and together they hoisted the large body up over the back of the mule. Looking up at the sky, he saw the clouds rolling past as the sprinkles died to nothing. Howell came out and observed the body, fingering his gun.

"I'll take him."

Daniel glanced up, eyebrows drawn together. "I'll go too."

"No, you stay and manage the camp."

His senses at alert, Daniel slowly relinquished the lead rope to Howell. Two men who had been in the other tent were called to go with him, something that made Daniel even more wary. But there was little he could do besides watch them head off in the mud, toward Matson.

The men returned to the tents to finish playing cards and resting. The ground was too wet to work. Daniel had no intention of trying to get them to dig. The wood was too damp to get a fire going so they supped on hard tack and jerky.

Daniel was edgy. He remembered Howell's face as he led the mule carrying John's body away. Something was up…but what?

****

The next morning, the ground had dried somewhat and the digging began in earnest. Daniel had cleared a large space out from under the tibia, and was now working around the other side. Anxiety rippled through him in an unnerving manner, as though a sword hung over his head by a threadbare rope.

As the sun hit its midway point, a shout went out and Daniel looked up to see Howell riding the mule while Sheriff Hancock was astride his black horse. Howell looked hard at Daniel, and a cold hand clenched his chest. The sheriff pulled out his rifle and swung down from his horse, then lifted the gun to point directly at Daniel. He froze.

The sheriff advanced slowly, rifle unwavering in its aim. "Daniel Bridger, I'm arresting you for the murders of Jim Smith, John Whelan, and Freddie MacMillan."

Chapter Fifteen

Elizabeth leaned against the door, for the second time in just a few days. She shook in ways she hadn't thought possible. What was this thing between her and Daniel, and why did it discombobulate her so?

Fido had stopped barking, so she reached down to fondle his ears and sigh. The chicks needed to be checked on, so she went outside to peer into their large crate. Seven little bodies huddled together in their roost. Their feathers had been coming in and she was surprised at how quickly they were growing.

The sun had gone down, the night sky had darkened and she stood, staring up at the starlit sky for a moment. Fido sat at her feet, head leaning against her knee. She stroked the furry head, then entered the house.

Daniel. His very name shivered her soul. How did he have such an effect upon her? He was tall, well-built, and had strong, even features. But there was something else besides the physical aspects of his person, there was his voice and the way he looked at her, as though she was the only person in the universe.

After scooting the chair closer, she stirred the fire with the poker, adding more wood to keep the blaze burning. Leaning back, she watched the flickering flames as they hesitated, then climbed slowly up the side of the log.

Her head tipped back as she thought about the violence over the past few weeks. Someone had killed Silent Jim, and then attacked Daniel on the trail to the site. Was there more to come?

Fido lay stretched out beside the fire and she went upstairs to undress for bed. Moonlight filtered through the single, small window and she lay in bed, watching the moonshadows shift about before finally falling asleep.

****

Sunlight poured in through the window, waking her early the next morning. She rose and dressed in her second-best dress and ate a hurried breakfast before tossing the leftovers between the dog and the chicks. Her mother came out and sighed, holding her head.

"Ma?"

"Don't worry, Lizzie. Just one of my headaches."

"Go lay down. I can handle everything."

Her mother sighed, then nodded. "I think you are right. Thank you." She disappeared back into her room.

Elizabeth straightened her skirt and headed out the door.

The town was quiet as she walked toward the museum. Mrs. Hutchins swept the sidewalk in front of the store, which reminded Elizabeth that the museum needed to be cleaned as well. After tying and pinning on her apron, she swept and dusted thoroughly. Then, she sat to work on the oreodont skull.

The morning went by, until Deputy Morley walked through the front door.

"Miss Ingram, a man died, possibly murdered, last night over by the Janney house. I know you were there yesterday and wondered if you saw anything."

"Murdered? But that's the second one—"

"This man's throat wasn't slit. So we don't know if it is the same assailant."

Elizabeth thought, then shook her head. "No. The only person I saw near the Janneys' was Daniel Bridger, and he was at my home. We discussed my father's work."

"Yes, I understand he is also a dinosaur digger. He works with the Howell crew, right? Working for Mayor Janney."

"Yes." Her voice tightened somewhat.

"A little professional rivalry there…"

"Not on our part."

"Well, please be careful."

"I recently acquired a dog, so I am well protected."

"That's good to hear." He left with another admonishment for her to be careful and she watched him go.

Murder! Since when was Matson a hotbed for the like? There had never been anyone killed before…Well, she had to amend that. Men had been killed in accidents, but never murder. What had happened to her little town?

For now, every creak of the building sent her looking to see if someone was there. Even the wind rattling the panes of the window accelerated her heartbeat. Though she hated to admit it… she was afraid.

Around midday she went home to eat something and feed her chicks. Fido jumped about, happy to see her, and she decided to take him with her when she returned. After some buttered bread and cheese, she headed back, with Fido on a rope.

The dog went around the room, sniffing and nosing into every corner and crevice. When he made his way back to her, she tied him to her chair and sat to work on her skull some more. The light bone was emerging ever so slowly from the darker matrix that surrounded it. She focused hard to keep from nicking the bone while she scraped the rock away. Time went by swiftly as she worked.

Someone ran by the museum's front, the boards clattering as he went. She rose and moved to the window to look outside, but did not see anything at first. But people were coming out of the shops to stand on the covered sidewalk. Then she saw it—Sheriff Hancock astride his black horse. Tied by a rope was a man pulled along the side. The man's hands were bound together and the rope was tied around the pommel of the saddle. He had obviously been walking a fair distance for he was dusty and windblown, the knees of his pants torn and bloody from where he had fallen.

It was Daniel.

She cried out, and immediately ran out of the museum. The crowd jeered and she asked Mrs. Hutchins what was happening.

"It's the killer. Sheriff caught him."

She mouthed the word "killer" and faded backward. The sheriff had reached the jail by now and swung down from his horse. He unlooped the rope from the saddle and led Daniel inside.

The crowd dispersed, and she waited until everyone had gone back to their shops, before stepping across the street into the one-room jailhouse.

She got there just as the iron door closed with a clang and the sheriff padlocked it shut. He frowned at her.

Daniel lifted his head slowly and said, "Miss Ingram, go home."

"I'm not leaving until I know what you have done."

"I've arrested him for the murders of three men. He's been in the vicinity of each one."

"That doesn't make him a killer."

"It makes him a suspect. He is right, though, you need to go home."

She looked at Daniel. "Did you do it? Look at me and answer."

He stared into her eyes and his voice was steely. "You know I didn't."

She nodded and turned to the sheriff. "You've got the wrong man. He's telling the truth."

He chuckled and went to pat her shoulder but she dodged his touch. "You need to just trust us to work this out. I know what I'm doing."

She turned an assessing eye upon the cell, taking in the simple cot and bare floor, with a pail in the corner. "Doesn't he get water to wash with, and a blanket? What about meals?"

The sheriff shrugged. "Mrs. Goode usually looks after the prisoners. I'll try to remember to tell her he's here."

Spinning on her heel, she sprinted across the street and down to her cabin, where she collected a bucket of water, a towel, a blanket, and some bread and cheese. All this she carried back to the jail. When she arrived, it was to find the sheriff gone.

Daniel's eyes widened when he saw her. "Damn it, Elizabeth, I told you to stay away."

Her chin lifted. "Just eat and drink. Put the blanket on the bed. You'll need it tonight. You can wash up a little bit, too."

She pushed the blanket through the bars, and the bread and cheese, which he devoured despite his protests. She lay the towel across the top of the bucket and set it and a small tin cup just outside the bars. He reached through and dipped up water, gulping it down in a single draught, then reached for more.

"Thank you, Miss Ingram."

"It was 'Elizabeth' a moment ago."

His head tilted to one side. "That was very wrong of me."

His wrists were raw from where the rope had bit into them. His clothes were dusty and torn from where he had fallen and been dragged at some point. His pants hung open at the knee where bloody flesh showed.

She leaned against the bars, and for some reason, tears smarted her eyes. Sniffling a little, she looked up. "Daniel, they hang murderers."

"I didn't do it. You must believe me."

"I do, but how do we get you out of here?"

"You find the person who did it."

"Me? How do I do that?"

"He'll strike again. Just be careful. Keep that damned dog with you."

"Miss Ingram, step away from the cell." The sheriff's voice cracked like a whip behind her.

Elizabeth jumped. Spinning, she breathed out and placed her hand on her bodice. "Really, Sheriff, was that necessary?"

"That there is a lying murderer, and you are far too close for comfort. I'm surprised at you; your father would be too."

Her chin went up. "I am not concerned with others' opinions of me."

Daniel broke in. "Thank you, Miss Ingram. You've been an angel of mercy. Now go. The sheriff is right."

She dusted off her skirt, only to realize she still wore her apron. Looking from one to the other, she said, "I'll bring supper in a while. You don't need to bother Mrs. Goode. Goodbye, Mr. Bridger."

Suddenly overcome with emotion, she walked away. In her mind's eye she kept seeing Daniel with a rope around his neck, hanging from a tree and her chest constricted. How to discover what was really happening?

Back at the museum, she petted Fido and let him out by tying him to the post out front while she swept off the sidewalk. She was sweaty by the time she finished, warmed by the heat of the day and exercise. Fido trotted at her heel when she went indoors and found himself a spot on the floor to lay down on.

Elizabeth sat at her work table, mind on anything but the oreodont skull. How to prove Daniel innocent? And why was she so sure? After all, he had deceived her when they met.

Her mind chewed on facts and memories while she scraped away at the matrix surrounding the skull. He had misrepresented himself when they first met, neglecting to tell either she or her father that he was employed by Janney and Howell. That he had spied on them, she was certain, but she was equally certain that he was drawn to her just as she was to him. But one didn't stick one's neck out on such evidence…did one?

Her head ached, and she realized a hairpin pulled

on her scalp. She drew it out. Her braid loosened, so she tugged out the rest until it lay dangling to the floor. Somehow, it did not hurt as much loose like this, though the weight of her hair still pulled. She stuck the hairpins in her apron pocket and left the braid hanging.

When the little clock struck four, she packed up her stuff and took hold of the dog's rope. After locking the door securely behind her, she trod along the sidewalk, her gaze drawn to the jail across the street.

The general store was nearly empty, and Mrs. Hutchins looked up immediately when she entered. Fido barked from where he had been tied up, but Elizabeth ignored him and went to the counter.

"I need some meat to fix for supper. And some potatoes and corn if you have any."

"Got some of both. What kind of meat?"

"Lamb, veal, or beef. Even a small portion of pork would be fine."

"Got some fresh lamb chops in. I'll pack you up some of them." She disappeared into the back room and reappeared with a paper containing four lamb chops, which she showed to Elizabeth before wrapping them up.

"Have you got any meat scraps?"

"That's right. Heard about your dog. Bad business with the hydrophoby around."

"He isn't sick. I've been watching."

Mrs. Hutchins disappeared again, returning with a packet she set on the counter next to the lamb chops. A few potatoes and a couple of ears of corn completed Elizabeth's purchase for the day. Then she had to hurry home to fix them in time to take Daniel supper.

She untied Fido after reaching home, then fed him

some of the meat scraps. The cabin felt a little cooler, and she went to the ewer to wash her face and hands. What to cook for supper?

Two hours later, she headed over to the jail with a covered plate in her hands. She'd left Fido eating some of his scraps so he would stay quietly at the cabin. When she reached the jail, it was empty and Daniel was lying on the cot.

"Ahem," she said and he jumped up.

"I'm sorry; I must have fallen asleep."

"It's fine. I just brought you some supper."

"How am I going to eat?"

"I'll stand here and you can reach through the bars to get your food from the plate."

He lifted up one of the lamb chops by the bone and took a bite. He cleaned the plate and she felt better, seeing that he had an appetite.

After he had drunk a cup of water, she said, "Has the sheriff said anything?"

"Just that they have enough information to hang me."

"But that isn't true!"

"It's his word against mine. And he is the law in these parts."

"What happened in the camp?"

"Man came down with rabies and Howell shot him. But he told the sheriff that I shot him. Sheriff needed someone for the other two deaths, so he fixed on me."

She sat in the chair and looked at him, standing there behind the bars. Her gaze fell on his torn knee. "Are you all right there?"

He looked down. "It looks worse than it is. I fell and the horse dragged me. I got it cleaned up."

"We just need to get you cleared."

"Your father may not like you consorting with me."

She shrugged away her father, doubting whether he would even notice. "Father is consumed by the *Camarasaurus*. I doubt it will come up." She picked up the plate. "I'll return in the morning."

"You don't have to do this."

"Yes, I do."

"Everyone will talk."

She smiled ruefully. "I am used to that."

The sky was darkening by the time she reached her home. Fido had finished eating and paced by the back door. She let him out and checked on the chicks, noting that something had been digging in a couple spots. After hunting out some rocks, she filled the holes, and lined the edges with more to make digging difficult. By then, Fido had returned and they went inside.

Chapter Sixteen

Daniel stared at the doorway where moments ago, Elizabeth had been. He was in a difficult place, and had no idea how to get out. Accused of murder, locked in a cell, and being ministered to by a darling of a woman whom he happened to be desperately in love with. What the hell?

He pushed away from the bars and sat heavily on the bed. It creaked and groaned, making him doubt whether it would hold up through the night. It was dark, and he wondered if he would even be given a candle.

A light swung into the jail as the door opened and Hancock strode in. He held up the lantern to examine Daniel and the cell. Seemingly satisfied, he set the lantern down on the chair and tried the lock. When it held, he nodded and turned away.

"You just going to leave me here?"

The sheriff turned to him. "Yep. Shore am."

Then he was gone, leaving Daniel in the musty room with the door shut and locked. There was only one window in the brick jail. It allowed only a little fresh air into the space, but at least he could see outside a little.

A dog barked in the distance, and he wondered if it were Elizabeth's dog. After the horrors of watching Big John die of rabies, he shuddered to think of her in the same position. If he'd had anything to say about it, the dog would simply have been shot. Or at least left out in the field to fend for itself. But she was too tenderhearted, it would seem.

The night grew cold quickly, and soon he had reason to bless Elizabeth for thinking to bring him a blanket. And food. And water. She'd thought of everything, except perhaps how to forgive him. He rolled up in the blanket and laid down on the cot. He had a long night ahead of him.

****

A day passed, and Thursday came. Elizabeth brought him some fresh bread and bacon for breakfast, but then hurried off to get a mule to carry supplies to her father's dig site. Sheriff Hancock shook his head when she headed off.

"That girl will never marry. She don't know her place."

"I think she does. She's far too intelligent to be stuck home cleaning and cooking. And yet, she does those as well."

"Those things need to be done by someone. Things are pretty evenly divided between the sexes."

Daniel disagreed. "I think women have a harder time of it in some respects. My mother, at least, would say so. Miss Ingram is ahead of her time."

"And as such, will never marry. You might have wanted her, but you're for the rope."

A shaft of icy fear pierced him. The sheriff stepped free of the jail and locked the door behind him. Daniel stared at the heavy wooden door. What could he do? How to escape execution?

He looked through the bars, out the single window. A shadow passed over it, backlit with sunshine, and a voice said, "Daniel Bridger?"

"Yes, who are you?"

"Enoch Darden. Looking for a crew to work on."

He frowned...What? "Haven't you heard? Bad luck this season."

"I think I'll tough it out. See you around."

The shadow disappeared, leaving Daniel confused. None of it had made sense. Who was Enoch Darden? The name was unfamiliar... though the voice was not. He wondered.

By the time the sun began to set over the mountains, Elizabeth was back. She hurried in with a covered lunch pail and set it down with a fresh bucket of water.

"Do you need anything?"

"An alibi..." the sheriff said from his chair.

She ignored him, looking directly at Daniel instead. He lifted the lid of the lunch pail and fished out the flatbread and jerky. "I brought it from the camp. Haven't had time to cook today."

"Thank you. I'm hungry enough to eat anything." And he was. He started eating when she motioned for him to go ahead.

"We have a new crew member, Enoch Darden."

He choked and looked up. "I met him... in a manner of speaking. He said he was looking for a crew. What does he look like?"

"I thought you knew him?" the sheriff said.

"I saw him once, not very well."

Elizabeth considered. "He's light haired, but I don't know that it's natural. And he has grayish eyes. Medium height and build."

"Could be anyone..."

"Yes. He claims to have experience, but I'm not sure. Father says he's fine, so I let it go."

"Strange that a mysterious character shows up this late in the season."

"Yes, but we can use him. The death in the other camp spooked a couple of our workers and they went back to their mines."

He thought for a moment about Big John's death and shuddered. It had been a horrible way to go. Her eyes softened and she reached out a hand through the bars.

Suddenly, the sheriff snatched her back from the cell. She stumbled and fell. Daniel surged against the bars, desperate to get to her, but he was trapped.

"I'm sorry, but don't touch the prisoner, miss. He's killed three men and might take you hostage." He pulled her to her feet.

She dusted off her dress and straightened. "I'll leave you then. Goodbye, Mr. Bridger, Sheriff." She was gone.

He gripped the bars and leaned his forehead against them. The sheriff went back to his seat and propped his boots up on the desk. Daniel gave the bars a shake and shoved backward to face the bare, stone wall of the jail. There was no way of busting out... not that escape would help his position. He needed to think things through.

Who could have committed the murders?

How would he find out, locked up in this cell?

Chapter Seventeen

Elizabeth fumbled with the ribbon of her bonnet and pulled it off as she stepped onto the porch of the cabin. Fido rose from the mat and stretched, trotting inside as soon as she opened the door. A little more wood to the fire and a quick check on the chicks which were beginning to fledge out, and she was ready to sit down and rest after a long day walking in the sun.

She filled a tin cup with water and sat in her chair beside the fire. Her legs ached from all the walking, and she was tired and sunstruck. On top of it all, she'd had to see Daniel in a low mood behind bars. What were they going to do?

They? As in she and Daniel? Her heart fluttered at the thought, then pounded its approval. So this was love, this aching, desperate need that could not be fulfilled.

She wasn't sure she liked it.

Fido whined and nosed into her hand. She patted his head and scratched him behind his ear. She was starting to feel hungry, but she didn't want to get up to make anything. But neither did she want to sit and brood. With a final pat to the dog, she went to the sourdough starter to mix up some bread for a late supper.

She carved a chunk of meat from the ham hanging up. It would soon be just a bare bone that she could use to flavor stock and beans. For now, though, there was enough for a few more meals at least. The spring chicks and fawns would have grown up soon enough that the hunters could go out again. Fresh grouse, quail and venison would be a welcome change.

After frying some onions and chopped ham together, she buttered the warm bread and sat at the table to eat. There was plenty, and she put a large helping into the lunch pail to take to Daniel. After a quick trip to the jail, she dropped it off with a shy smile and left before he could say anything beyond his thanks. She did not breathe until she was outside the jail.

Back at home she set aside some food for breakfast, then fed Fido the rest of the bread and ham. He was starting to fill out nicely and his fur was thickening up, giving him a more rounded appearance. He looked younger, and she smiled to see it.

The door opened and her mother came in, shed her shawl and sat heavily beside the fire. "Little Larry Boone died. The mother is absolutely grief struck. We got her some laudanum and put her to bed."

"Oh, poor thing!"

"Yes, it was rather horrible. Thank you for cooking, Lizzie."

"Of course, Ma."

"I heard about Mr. Bridger. And to think we were harboring a killer all that time."

"I don't think he did it, Ma."

Mrs. Ingram stopped fanning herself. "Why not?"

What to say? "He has assured me he is innocent. I've been taking food to him."

"Elizabeth! Taking food to an unmarried man?

People will talk!"

"Ma...you know I don't care about that. He's innocent, and I'm going to do what I think is right."

They stared at one another for a moment, before her mother sighed and leaned back in defeat. "I know you will. Just be careful, Lizzie."

"I will, Ma."

She wanted to read the latest paleontology journal of papers, but she had torn her dress on a thorny bush that day and falling backward at the jail had not helped. It needed to be repaired before it was washed, and she was doing laundry the next day.

That meant going upstairs, slipping out of everything and into the dressing gown, then coming back down to sew beside the fire. Huffing slightly, she pushed up from the chair to do it.

As she sewed the tiny stitches that, hopefully, would not show too much, she thought again about Daniel. There was some mystery around him, and she wondered what it was.

Despite the fact that she was sure he was not completely honest about himself, she still felt drawn to him. Hopefully it would not end badly. She thought of the numerous ways it could go wrong and a tear leaked out. She breathed deeply and dashed it away. All would be well; she had to believe that.

Mending done, she patted Fido, kissed her ma's cheek, and went upstairs to bed. The night was cool, and the sky outside was clear. As she sat and stared at the stars, one fell and streaked across the night.

She made a sudden wish, then felt foolish for the childish notion. Turning her gaze down the street to the little stone jail, she leaned against the glass and closed her eyes with the fervor of her hopes.

****

Morning came, filled with work. She had to take Daniel some breakfast, and go to the general store to get a few things. After eating a few quick bites, she packed the rest in a pail and carried it over to the jail.

It was still locked, so she looked in the window to see him lying on the bed, staring up at the ceiling. He glanced over, and a slow smile spread across his face. He rolled up to a sitting position.

"You don't need to do this."

"If I don't feed you, who will? The whole town thinks you're a murderer."

"You don't need to be branded by me."

"I won't, but surely people won't deny you food."

Footsteps approached and she looked up to see the sleepy face of the sheriff. His breath still had the faintest taint of alcohol.

"There you go, feed your lost puppy."

"He's no puppy. He's a man. Surely we are commanded to feed the destitute and visit the prisoners."

He grunted and sat heavily, groaning as he leaned his head back. "Feed him and go. I need it quiet."

Elizabeth handed him the lunch pail and picked up the other. She mouthed "Goodbye" and left.

The general store was crowded, but fell silent as she entered. People gave her a wide berth as they gathered their purchases and left. Soon she was left alone with Mrs. Hutchins. That lady did not smile at her, simply stood behind the counter and watched her approach.

Frowning a little, Elizabeth said, "I need a few

things, Mrs. Hutchins."

"That will be cash up front, Miss Ingram."

Elizabeth's mouth dropped open in astonishment. But rather than argue, she dug in her pocket to see how much money she had in hand. She laid the coins on the counter. "One sack of potatoes, a cake of yeast, a bag of flour, some sugar, and I need some lard if there's enough. Can Timothy bring them to me?"

"Tim, here Tim." A tow-headed youth of about thirteen peered through the doorway.

"Yeah, Ma."

"Get a sack of potatoes and one of flour and take them down to the Ingrams, then come back for the rest."

He looked at Elizabeth, then back at his mother before saying, "Yes, Ma."

Mrs. Hutchins pushed a single coin across to her. She pocketed it, then left with her cheeks burning.

Tim carried the bags of potatoes and flour as far as her door. Where once he would have offered to carry them into her kitchen, he set them down beside her mat and went back for the rest. She was left to drag the bags across to her kitchen, where she leaned them up against the wall.

When she had finished bringing in her groceries, she sat and cried for a moment, hot, angry tears. The town had turned on her... all for feeding an outlaw.

An outlaw who was innocent.

Well, they could not stop her. She would do what she knew to be right, regardless of the outcome. She made some salt bread and fried it up in the fresh lard she had bought, stacking it up on her mother's favorite blue and white plate. After tossing Fido a piece of flatbread, she sliced some cheese, and headed back to the jail.

Janney's shadow Will Gunn stood outside the jail and stopped her from entering. The sheriff's and the mayor's voices blended together, though she could not understand much of what they were saying. Had they forgotten that Daniel was there and could hear them?

She took the moment to study Janney's mysterious manservant at close quarters. He was roughly shaven, with a pocked face. His skin was tanned and leathery from long days in the sun. He looked as though his face would crack if he tried to smile.

Without looking at her, he let her know he was watching her. She stood patiently until Mayor Janney came out, and the shadow man fell soundlessly into place behind him. Elizabeth entered, to find the sheriff looking flustered. He waved her over to the cell and she carried the plate of fried bread and cheese to Daniel.

"What is all this… How did you know I love fried bread?"

She tried to smile. "Doesn't everyone?"

But he barely looked at her and he did not eat much.

"What's wrong?"

He shook his head and glanced up at the sheriff, who stood there watching. "Nothing. But could you get a message to someone?"

"Of course. Tell me."

"His name is Matthew Mattis, of Winslow Place, Philadelphia. Just send him a note detailing the trouble I am in."

"Of course. I will do that today. Matthew Mattis, of Winslow Place."

"Yes."

"I'll go now and take care of it." They shared a look, and he gave her a slight smile.

Elizabeth all but ran home to leave the plate and write out a quick note. Then she had an idea. The telegraph lines had come with the train. Perhaps she should send the message that way. She carried her note to the telegraph office with her last few coins and with the help of the telegrapher, tailored it down to the fewest possible letters. She listened as the telegraph was sent, sounding almost like a song with the rhythm of the tapping. By then the sun was high in the sky and it was too late to begin laundry.

Instead, she went to the museum to work on the skull. The focus helped take her mind off the morning's treatment by the townsfolk. Nothing they did would make her stop believing in Daniel. Would it?

A final chip with the pick and the lower jaw was free. She spent a moment looking at the ivory-colored teeth, imagining the creature when it was alive. That it was a herbivore was clear by the grinding surface of the premolars and molars and the shearing action of the incisors. She ran her thumb along the smooth surface of the jaw and set it down.

She closed up and locked the door, then turned toward home. The street was nearly empty of people, leaving her way clear. Fido rose from the mat when she got home and wagged his tail as he slipped inside the cabin. It was getting late, and she needed to take something to Daniel for supper.

A few minutes later and the smell of cornbread baking in the Dutch oven filled the cabin. She swept as it cooked, then checked on the chicks. They were bigger every day, scratching and pecking at the ground, and soon she would trust them to forage around the back of the cabin for insects and seeds. Fido had caught a prairie dog and was eating it next to the back door. She averted her eyes from the bloody mess and went inside.

After determining the cornbread was done, she pulled the oven off the coals and cut a large piece to cool, and take to the jail. There was some milk in the can, although she would need to get some more soon. Her butter was getting low...

The desertion by the town had hurt her, and she didn't know what to do about it. Unless Daniel was proven innocent, how would she and her parents be able to stay in a town that had turned against them? Perhaps she needed to discuss it with her father...

She wrapped the cornbread in a napkin and picked up the jug of milk to take to the jail. As before, the street was nearly empty of people, just a lone rider on a horse going through town.

The jail was open, but the sheriff was gone when she got there. Daniel rolled up from the bed and came to the bars.

"You came."

"Of course." She handed over the cornbread and milk. "Why wouldn't I?"

"Sheriff told me people might turn against you."

"Mmm. He might have had something to do with that. Never mind, I can handle it."

"You shouldn't have to."

She sighed. "No. But when we show you didn't do this, they'll change their minds."

"If we can... I don't know what can be done."

She reached through the bars and put her hand on his arm. "We will, somehow. You have to believe that."

He looked at her, eyes sorrowful. "Trying."

"I will need to go out to the site for a day or two. I'll make sure Mrs. Goode brings you food."

He nodded. "You be careful."

"I will."

He reached for her, catching her hand before she withdrew it. Her mouth parted in surprise as he pulled her closer, then ever so slowly bent toward her until their lips met through the bars. A flood of warmth and wonder rushed through her. Even as he set her free, his gaze still held her. Her hand fell away to her side and she hesitated, before finally turning away.

The walk home was a blur. Even Fido running in circles around her feet could not break the spell. Her heart hammered in her chest, and her mind whirled. She must get him free...

She went to Mrs. Goode's and wrung a reluctant agreement to provide two meals a day for Daniel from her. Once home, she checked her pack, deleting and adding items as she saw fit, before finally retiring to bed. Her ma came home as she set her pack by the back door and huffed.

"Going off in the morning?"

"I need to see if they know anything. Can you remember to check on the chicks? I'll leave them plenty of feed."

"I'll keep an eye on your babies."

****

Early the next morning, she set off. The chicks had a large pile of food to get them through the next couple of days, and Fido was choosing to come with her. She hoped to get there quickly so she could talk to her father about what was happening.

The day was warm and she was hot and dusty by the time she reached the creek beside the camp. She ignored the temptation to strip down to undergarments and immerse herself in the cool, clear water. Instead, she simply drank and washed up before turning to the camp. Sounds of hammer strikes could be heard and a shout now and then.

One of the men caught sight of her and hailed her father. He turned, frowned as he focused, then a broad grin spread across his face as he set down his hammer. They had uncovered even more of the cervical vertebra and she peered ahead to see where they were at the moment.

Her father pulled her into a brief hug. "I wasn't expecting you for two more days. It isn't Thursday."

"Father, Daniel has been arrested for murder. He is in the jail. I've been taking him meals, but that seems to have angered the townspeople. Mrs. Hutchins insisted on cash up front."

"There's the money in the concordance…"

She shook her head. "It's gone. I thought you had used it."

"No, I would remember that, surely?"

They were quiet for a moment; only the banging of hammers and picks could be heard.

He patted her shoulder. "Is that why you're here?"

Nodding, she said, "I thought you should know about the townsfolk."

"I am sorry for that, and I hope it isn't true about Mr. Bridger."

"I can't help but think there is something else we

don't know going on."

"What could it be? Rival groups, and he chose the other side over us. After first ingratiating himself to us. What could it be except that he's a spy?"

"My heart tells me…"

"Your head, Elizabeth, what does your head tell you?"

She lifted her head. "That even if he was a spy, he doesn't deserve to hang."

"And if he killed those men? What then?"

She bit her lip to keep from crying out. Instead, she reached for a hammer and chisel before picking a spot on the neck of the *Camarasaurus* and settling in to work. Out of the corner of her eye, she saw her father shaking his head and fought against tears that pressed forward.

The afternoon passed slowly, despite the industry with which she applied herself to the task. By the time the day was called, she had nearly completely removed the vertebra from the ground. She set the tools aside and went to wash up for supper. Charlie had been cooking all afternoon and she wondered what he had come up with.

One of the men had shot a couple of grouse, and to the meat from those birds, Charlie had added some dumplings. This had stewed long enough to thicken the broth into gravy and the result was wonderful. The men and Elizabeth inhaled it, until there was none left over.

"Charlie," she asked, "Where did you learn to cook?"

He shrugged, looking down. "My ma. Said I'd never find a woman who'd have me so I'd need to know how to feed myself."

"Well, you cook like this for some woman and she'll snatch you up," she said, chuckling.

He smiled, shooting her a shy look, before returning to his study of the ground.

She looked around and frowned. A face was missing. "Where is the new man? He asked me and I sent him along several days ago. Enoch something."

"Darden? He came. Asked a bunch of questions then disappeared."

Night closed over them, and a blanket of high clouds kept the stars from showing themselves. The moon was a glowing smear behind the thin clouds, giving little light to the world below. Elizabeth crawled into her bedroll and tried to ignore the numerous small points of pressure from the ground. Fido curled up against her back, his warmth welcome in the cool night. Her mind scattered, making her think she would never sleep. Exhaustion won out, and she fell asleep.

****

She worked until noon the next day, finally freeing the vertebra and adding it to the pile of bones ready to be transported back to Matson. For that they would need to rent a cart and a pair of mules, and she wondered if anyone would work with them now.

"Snake!"

She looked up, scouting for the source of the shout. It was one of the new men and he stood stock-still, staring at something on the ground in front of him. Henry pulled out a pistol, which he leveled at the snake. It hissed and rattled, ready to strike, until the bullet struck its head. It thrashed wildly.

Morty took his pick and pressed it down so someone could cut the head off, and it was quickly buried. Charlie took charge of the body and began preparing it. Elizabeth had eaten rattlesnake once before, and though not her favorite meat, found it perfectly edible.

As the sun set on her second day back at the work site, she wondered how Daniel was doing. Who was the Matthew Mattis he had asked her to write to? Why had he wanted the message sent?

She joined the rest of the men gathered at the kettle for some rattlesnake stew. Charlie had cooked the snake with potatoes and carrots. They all spent some time picking bones from their plates, but it was tasty.

The next morning she rose stiff and sore from sleeping on the rocky ground. She tried to pick up the vertebra she had chipped free the day before, but it was far too heavy for her to carry. It would have to wait with the rest of the bones.

She hugged her father and lifted her pack to head home. The sun had just risen above the mountain, spreading light into the gulley and onto the dig. Elizabeth was about to leave when an explosion rocked the gulley.

A thunderous slide of rocks and gravel spilled into the creek some ways up the rise. Everyone sprinted to see what had happened. Barking, Fido ran at her heels, and they dodged boulders and sliding gravel until they came to the smoking section of the gulley.

There, they found a large section of the mountain blown apart. There was no sign of anyone else, and no possible reason found for the explosion. Confused, they filtered back to the work site when suddenly someone raced up the path, waving his arms.

"Get back, it's gonna blow!" he shouted.

An explosion ripped through their dig site. She huddled under Daniel's body as rocks, gravel, and bones rained down upon them. Before the dust had cleared, her father cried out and dashed to where the *Camarasaurus* had been.

Elizabeth stared at Daniel. "It is you! How did you get free? How did you know?"

He hesitated, then said, "Your telegram to Mattis got me free for now. I heard Janney talking about something happening here and came to warn you."

Her gaze was torn away by another cry from her father. She disentangled herself and ran to his side over rubble and boulders to where the dinosaur had lain.

It was destroyed.

A few of the larger bones looked mostly intact, but they had been thrown about. The smaller bones of the upper portion of the *Camarasaurus* were pulverized and scattered over a wide radius. She reached for her father's hand and squeezed it as he stood staring dumbly at the sight. For all practical purposes, it was gone.

The men arrived one by one and stood together with them. Daniel was suddenly there beside her, and she reached for his hand. He took it in his large and warm one, and she felt a little safer for the moment.

Looking up at him, she asked, "What happened?"

"Dynamite. I heard them talking about it just outside the mayor's house. They didn't know I'd been let out. I hurried as fast as I could, but I wasn't fast enough."

"How did you get out of jail?"

"Got a lawyer from Denver to argue for my release based on lack of evidence."

"So you're free then?"

"Not quite. I'm still under suspicion… and this will only heighten that." He sighed.

"How did you get the lawyer?"

He hesitated. "Matthew Mattis arranged it."

"Who is he?"

One of the men suddenly shouted, "There's an injured man here!"

Chapter Eighteen

Daniel sprinted over the uneven ground to where the man lay bleeding from a gash on his head. He recognized him from the Howell crew. Brandt, he thought his name was. He found a jagged stone with a bloody mark and a few hairs on one of its edges.

"This is what struck him. He was too close to the blast."

"Do you think he set it off?" asked Henry.

"Might have. Or, might have just been in the wrong place at the wrong time."

Elizabeth knelt beside the man. "Quick, fetch the first aid kit."

Moments later it was set down next to the injured man while she went to the creek to dampen a cloth. When she came back, she cleansed the wound and applied some pressure to stop the bleeding. After a few minutes, she bandaged it up as his eyes fluttered open. He frowned as he focused on her.

"You're the Ingram girl," he said.

"Yes, I am."

"What happened?"

"There was an explosion and you were injured."

He closed his eyes and frowned. "Can't be. Too far away."

"Well, here you lay with a deep laceration to your head," she said matter-of-factly.

He was silent, and Daniel thought perhaps he had passed out again. Dr. Ingram still stared at the wreck of his fossils. He nodded to one of the men.

"Get a blanket. We need to move him closer to the fire."

Moments later the blanket arrived and they spent a tense few minutes loading him onto it. Then three other men grabbed a corner and the four of them transported Brandt to the circle around the fire. He had a canteen attached to his belt, and Daniel sent a man off to fill it at the creek.

Elizabeth followed with the first aid kit. She set it down beside the injured man and looked up at Daniel. Her dog had still not returned from running off after the explosion. She glanced up at the sky and said, "I need to get home. Ma will worry. I hope she remembers to feed the chicks."

"The chicks?"

"I have some chicks... Well. they will be pullets soon. I need to get home."

"I don't like you walking home alone."

"I'll have Fido."

"Do you see him?"

She searched the land surrounding them for a moment, then shook her head. "No, I don't. I can't leave him."

"Stay one more night. The chicks can last that long."

Her mouth compressed, but she nodded shortly. Her gaze slid to her father, and soon she rose and went to him. After waiting for a few minutes, he followed.

"What are we going to do?" Dr. Ingram said to Elizabeth.

Her hands pressed his arm. "We will finish the dig."

"Elizabeth, look around you. There's nothing here."

She huffed. "I see a nearly intact femur; there lies the tibia in three pieces, with the foot encased still in its rock matrix. The neck vertebrae, I grant you, are probably lost to us, as are the scapulae. But we may recover the upper limbs to a degree. And, there is always the possibility that the skull is there."

He took a deep breath, and lifted tear-stained eyes. "Yes, yes. We will carry on, of course." He turned to Daniel and his expression hardened. "Sir, I do not know what to do with you. On one hand, you have deceived us. And on the other we owe you our lives."

"I can only say that I have always had your best interests at heart. You must believe me."

"It is difficult. But for now, I have no choice but to rely on you again." He held out his hand, and Daniel grasped it with both of his.

"You will not regret this, sir," he said.

Elizabeth was poking around, picking up debris from time to time and setting them back down after looking at them. She wandered along what had been the neck of the sauropod. She straightened and said, "Father, the damage is less here. I see an untouched vertebra, and the rock here is split now. I see bone!"

Dr. Ingram took a step, and then another, until he was nearly running. Half stumbling over the rocky ground, he stopped beside her and pulled out a mirror to angle light down onto the rock. After whipping out his magnifying glass, he peered down and with an excited shout cried, "An occiput! It is the skull!"

Despite the tragedy, there was an air of celebration that evening as they ate the ham and peas that Charlie had prepared for them. Daniel arranged to sit beside Elizabeth, but found her silent and withdrawn. But then, their site had been bombed—who wouldn't be withdrawn?

Their injured guest had wakened somewhat and taken some water. He was not awake enough to answer questions as yet, and Daniel suspected he was pretending to be more befuddled than he was to avoid them. Instead, he looked at the woman sitting beside him.

"Miss Ingram?" he said.

"Yes?"

"I have not yet thanked you for your kindness to me when I was imprisoned."

"Oh... I would have done the same for anyone."

"Who?"

"What?"

"Who have you ministered to in jail?"

"I... no one up to now."

"Well, I thank you for your kindness to me."

Her eyes widened, and her voice was low as she said, "You were most welcome."

He nearly kissed her, but there were people about. Still, her gaze flicked to his lips, and he knew she thought of it, too. For now, her staring at him would have to be enough.

"Tomorrow, we will shift focus. We need to clean up the site, clear the debris, and gather up what bone fragments we can find. We may be able to piece some bones together." Dr. Ingram said.

"We need to extract the skull as well. Before

anything else happens," Elizabeth said.

"It is safe enough where it is. We must clean up the site and put it to rights first."

Elizabeth was not comfortable with that assessment, and he could see her point of view. The field had not been a safe place for their fossils so far this season.

A barking in the distance broke the loud hum of voices and he reached out for her, only to find she had heard it too.

She stood and called out, "Fido! Here, boy!"

The barking grew louder, and soon there was a wiggling, whining dog at Elizabeth's feet. She patted him and ruffled his ears, obviously happy to have him back. Daniel was relieved too, for she would have some protection on her walk back to the town the next morning.

****

The sun was hidden the following day by a thick bank of clouds. Elizabeth packed her things and fed some flatbread to Fido before they headed out. She seemed to be avoiding him, despite his attempts to talk to her. He managed only a single shared glance before she shouldered her pack and headed out.

Dr. Ingram had regained his sense of purpose overnight and began by organizing them into work groups to focus on tasks. Daniel was put with Dr. Ingram to decide between rock and bone amongst the debris. It was sorted into baskets that were then carried off and dumped—rock and loose gravel in the ravine, bone spread on tarps outside the camp.

They worked until the rain began to fall, then they dragged their bedrolls under the overhanging slab of rock. They had carried the injured Howell crewmember under the shelter as well, and he seemed able to sit up now, though he leaned back against the rock wall with his eyes closed, discouraging conversation. He especially seemed to avoid Daniel.

The day dragged by. Inactivity gnawed at him, and he wished he had something to whittle like a few of the other men did.

The rain ended in the middle of the afternoon, and the men emerged from under the hanging rock to pick up their tools once more. With most of the debris cleared, the hole made by the dynamite was clear. More than one head turned toward the injured crewman, and the whispering grew louder.

Finally, Daniel went and sat beside the man. He was silent for a few moments before saying, "I saw you with Howell's crew, but I don't remember your name."

The man huddled in his blanket. "Amos."

"Amos…Brandt?"

"Yes."

"How did you come to be at this camp just as the explosives went off?"

"Maybe I come to warn 'em. What are you doing here?"

"This is just where I am," he said vaguely.

A smile crept up on the other's face. "Well, same here I guess. Now hush, my head hurts."

Daniel moved away, unsatisfied with what he had learned. He was now more than positive Amos had set the explosives. The question was, what to do with that? He was too injured to set loose, and the longer he stayed, the greater the chance they would get more information from him.

They slept that night crowded under the rock overhang on the only dry ground in the area. By the next morning, it had dried enough for them to begin work in earnest. Dr. Ingram was nearly back to his old self... Nearly. There was a shadow over him that nothing could dispel.

In the early afternoon, a shout went up. Daniel wiped a hand across his sweaty, gritty brow and stood to see what was happening. He saw the sheriff's hat and felt a moment of panic. Breathing deeply, he calmed his rapidly beating heart and bent down to lift the humerus fragment. The sheriff talked with Dr. Ingram, the latter pointing out the damage done by the explosion. He focused on work for a while, until a familiar voice broke in.

"Here you are, Bridger."

"Sheriff."

"Your lawyer's been all over Matson, saying you were improperly charged and all that."

"I am grateful to him."

"And now, as soon as you are released, the Ingram crew experiences an explosion that damages the site."

"Where'd the dynamite come from?"

"Matson's a mining town. Ain't that difficult to find."

"No, I mean where did this dynamite come from? I happen to know the Howell crew had dynamite on site."

"Why would they want to damage fossils?"

Daniel stood, and for the first time realized he was taller than the sheriff. "Crews can be adversarial and competitive. This find was a superior one to the Howell dinosaur."

"I think you had something to do with it, and I'm

gonna find a way to prove it."

"Maybe you should talk to Amos Brandt over there. He's one of the Howell crew and was injured in the explosion."

"He's next on the list. But remember, I got my eye on you."

Daniel nodded and bent again to pick up a bone fragment. Sheriff Hancock moved over to where Brandt sat alone beside the fire. He crouched for a few minutes in deep discussion with the man, before rising and raising his hat in Dr. Ingram's direction. Then he headed off down the trail toward Matson.

Daniel breathed a sigh of relief. He was still free... for now.

They slept around the fire that night, under a clear sky. His muscles and back ached from bending and lifting rocks, fossils, debris off the ground. Now, more stones pressed into him from the ground under one of his blankets. He didn't think he would ever sleep.

He must have, for late in the night he snapped awake. Something, or someone, had touched him and he surged up from under his covers.

"Shhh, settle down." The glow of the embers did not reach to the stranger's face.

"Who are you?"

"My name is Darden. I need to warn you; Howell isn't through with you."

"What more can he do? Shoot us?"

"It may come to that. You need to be aware."

"Why are you doing this?"

"Now ain't the time. I have to go." He melted away into the darkness, leaving Daniel with more questions than answers.

****

Morning found him groggy. He'd had a difficult time sleeping after his midnight visitor, and now felt stiff from lying on the ground. He had forgotten to ask the sheriff if Elizabeth had made it home all right, but doubted he'd have gotten much of an answer from him. Anxiety shot through him when he thought of her, and that made his nerves even more taut.

Sunshine shone down through a clear, brilliant blue sky. Daniel found himself watching the periphery for any signs of danger. A lone coyote loped along the ridge above them at some point and he studied it to see if it behaved strangely. But it simply paused long enough to look them over before hastening away.

Dr. Ingram came to him after lunch, "Daniel, I want you to take over the work on the back of the skull."

Daniel's mouth dropped open, and he hurriedly closed it. "Sir, I don't know that I have the skill for that."

"Next to Elizabeth, yours are the hands I trust best and I need to start piecing some of these bone fragments together."

"All right, sir, I'll do my best."

Dr. Ingram walked away, shoulders still hunched as though in defeat. He sent out a silent wish that all this would somehow come right.

Chapter Nineteen

"Elizabeth? Elizabeth!" her mother shouted up the stairs toward the loft.

Elizabeth shot up from bed and dragged her dressing gown on before running down the steps. "What is wrong?"

"Your chickens! They're all over the yard and at this rate the foxes or hawks will get them."

She ran outside and found her mother was right. Pullets were everywhere, scratching and pecking quite happily. But the day was warming, and soon the hawks would be up in the sky, riding thermals as they hunted.

One at a time she collected them and replaced them in the crate after blocking the hole they had escaped through. She straightened and sighed. She would need a proper chicken coop. Unfortunately, no one in town would help her, and her father was out in the field.

"Ma, what are we going to do with them? This crate is getting too small."

"Maybe should have thought of that before getting a passel of chicks?"

"Yes, maybe."

She knew where her father's hammer was, and she knew that nails came from the blacksmith. They had a pile of various boards and a saw, something she had used before when breaking apart old crates for firewood. Surely a coop couldn't be that hard to construct?

For now, she needed to help her ma with the laundry. The large tub was already outside over the fire and Elizabeth joined her mother in carrying water from the rain barrel to the tub. When the water was hot, they began.

She hated laundry. She hated everything about it. From the way her hands went raw from accidentally rubbing on the washboard, to how the soap burned in the numerous nicks and cracks in her hands from working in the field. It was hot, sweaty, damp work, and she was just glad that she would get a bath that evening.

By the time the sun was overhead, the lines were filled with clothes and sheets billowing in the breeze. She helped her mother pour out the water and together they carried the tub into the cabin to use for their baths that evening.

"I'm going to try and build a better coop."

"That's fine, Lizzy. I have to go check on the McAllisters. I don't know when I'll be back." Her mother attached a collar to her dress and laid her apron over the arm carrying her basket. She patted her hair into place and stepped out the door.

Elizabeth went out to the temporary chicken coop and thought. She could see what she wanted in her head, but making that a reality might prove difficult. First, though, she needed to go get some nails.

The blacksmith was on the opposite edge of town. She changed into her best dress and actually put on a bonnet. She gathered her shopping basket and headed out.

The town was busy. It was interesting to see how

many ways people could stare at her and yet avoid her gaze. She ignored them, simply striding across the street, avoiding the horses and wagons as she went, then walking on the opposite sidewalk toward the smithy.

It was a large place, with two boys who worked the bellows for the furnace. Just now they sat eating cornbread while Mick Johnson, the blacksmith, talked to a well-dressed man from out of town. The man finally nodded and left, leaving Mick to look at her. He was a powerfully built man.

He cocked his head and said, "Well, miss, what do you need?"

"I need some nails to build a chicken coop."

"Penny a bag."

She dug in her pocket, pulled out the coin, and he snapped his fingers to the boys. One jumped up and went into the house attached to the smithy. He returned with a small burlap bag that he handed to her. She handed him the penny and he closed her hand back over it.

"You keep it. I think you were brave to help out the man in the jail."

Her mouth dropped open. "You do?"

"I was wrongly accused once myself." He nodded to her and turned back to his forge, leaving her to bemusedly head for home. Halfway there, she thought she would stop into the museum. As she neared it, her senses were heightened, and her pace accelerated. The door swung on its hinges, the lock pried open with something heavy and powerful. She dashed inside, and dropped her basket.

Streaks and splashes of whitewash lay everywhere,

interspersed with splatters of blacking. Bones were cracked and smashed in their trays. She ran to her work table and halted.

The oreodont had been shattered.

Tears burst forth as she beheld the beautiful skull in fragments. She picked up the chair and set it right, then sat, staring at the mess before her. She looked up as the door opened. Her mother stood there.

"I heard from Mrs. McAllister." She touched a broken fossil and sighed. "Can anything be salvaged?"

Elizabeth sniffed and tried to wipe her eyes. Her mother placed a handkerchief in her hand and she started to dry her face, only to break down again. Her mother rubbed her back in a soothing circular pattern. She did not speak, simply stood beside her as she cried.

After a few minutes, Elizabeth lifted her head and dabbed her eyes and nose. She was numb, broken beyond feelings.

"Elizabeth."

"Mama," she croaked out.

"Come, child. We need to go home."

"I can't… I can't leave them like this."

"Lizzy, they're bones. They will wait for you and your father to set them to rights."

She sniffed. "We can't lock the door."

"I'll put a sign up that the museum is closed and for people to stay out."

"A locked door didn't keep *them* out. Why would a sign?"

"Lizzy, just come home."

She pushed herself up from the table, then reached out to touch the pale bone at the back of the skull, the only piece of any size to remain. After swallowing, she picked up her basket, and followed her mother.

****

For two days she stayed indoors. Fido came and went; the pullets squabbled, but she made no effort to expand the coop. She churned butter when her mother asked her, chopped wood for the fire, and sewed as needed. But when her mother went to the general store for some supplies, Elizabeth stayed home.

At the end of the two days, her mother came to her. "Lizzy, put the knitting aside and look at me."

Elizabeth sighed and set the needles down. "Yes, Ma?"

"You can't go on like this. Grieve and be done. But there's plenty of life left to live."

"The people hate us, Ma."

"Mrs. Hutchins and Lydia were right pleasant to me."

"All right, they hate me."

"A couple, maybe a few, may do. But there are lots of folks in this town, and some of them like you."

"But, Ma, the oreodont...! How could someone destroy it? It will never come again."

"There will be more skulls, Lizzy."

"But, Ma—"

"No, Lizzy, hear me. I know it was precious to you. And I even understand why. I've been married to your father long enough to see that. Remember, my father was a museum curator back east."

That was something she so often forgot. Her face lifted. "What are we going to do, Ma?"

"We're going to continue to do what we have always done. We're late getting a garden in, that's something. We need to build a coop for the chickens. I don't rightly know how we'll do that, but we'll figure it out. We have plenty of sewing to do; in a few months we'll be harvesting food from our garden. And you'll have specimens to clean and prepare."

She nodded, though she could not give the smile she knew her mother wanted. "Yes, Ma."

"Now, goodness knows when your father will return. How he can sleep outdoors at his age! We've got the floors to scrub after all that rain."

"Oh, Ma!"

"No, I mean it. It will do you good. Go put your light green work dress on and I'll get the bucket of suds ready."

By the time the floor was clean, Elizabeth's knees and hands were raw. But she had to admit that she felt better and that the house certainly looked better. As she sat beside the fire, resting with the latest journal on paleontology on her lap, she felt instead a deep longing to see Daniel again.

Fido pushed his nose into her hand and she half-smiled, rubbing his ears and scratching his cheek. The shaken feeling she'd had since the assault on the museum was now gone, leaving a deep emptiness that nothing seemed to fill, except perhaps the memory of Daniel's kiss.

The sun shone outside as she sorted through the planks and scrap lumber to see what she could put together for her chicken coop. The large crate they were in right now would work for a night time roost, though she would need a door for it so she could lock them up at night. She let the pullets forage while she worked in the sunshine, with Fido lying stretched out to watch them.

By the time the sun settled over the mountains again, she had built a high yard out of somewhat mismatched boards. The box crates were arranged within to act as a roost within a shelter for the birds. An old crock of water and a pan of feed lay in the yard, and she had spread some straw from an old bale around in the crate. It wasn't the most professional of jobs, but she was proud of it.

"Elizabeth, supper is ready," her mother called out the back door.

"Coming, Ma," she said.

"I've got to go out to check on the McAllisters. I don't know when I'll be back."

Elizabeth dished up a piece of the flatbread her mother had made and paired it with a piece of cheese. A journal lay on the table, and she opened it up to an article on a fossil cave site out in Montana. She only noticed it was getting dark when it became difficult to read.

Her mother still wasn't home, so she fed the fire, and lit a couple of lanterns to read by. When she had finished reading all the articles in the magazine, she went to the chair by the fire and stared at the flickering flames.

It still hurt—the destruction of the museum combined with her feelings for Daniel. Somehow, they needed to figure out what was happening, and how to find a way to each other. If, that is, he even wanted her.

His actions said that he did, but had she not heard of men toying with the affections of young women? It wasn't as though they could have anything that resembled a normal courtship. How was she to know where she stood with him?

By the time the clock tolled nine, her mother still wasn't home, so she made sure Fido was settled beside the fire and climbed the stairs to the loft. It was with relief that she loosed her corset and climbed into bed wearing only her shift. Her last thoughts before falling asleep were of Daniel.

The next morning was cloudy, heavy with the threat of rain. She dressed in her second-best dress and went downstairs. Her mother's gentle snores came from the bedroom, so she stoked the fire as quietly as she could and started some gruel in the pot.

By the time it was ready, her mother came out of her room wrapped in her voluminous dressing gown. Her long braid dangled down her back and she pulled it out of the way before sitting at the table. Elizabeth served up some of the gruel for her mother and pushed over the butter and sugar.

"Thank you, Lizzie. I'm sorry I slept so late."

"You probably didn't get home til sometime this morning."

"I believe the clock struck two at some point after I got home."

"How are the McAllisters?"

After a pause, her mother said, "The baby died. The rest of the family is better, though."

"Oh no. How many is that for them?"

"Three, in as many years."

Elizabeth sat in silence, contemplating the loss of three children to illness and accident.

"When is the funeral?"

"I don't know. I'm sure they will let us know."

With a sigh, Elizabeth rose. She collected rags, a scrub brush, and the bar of soap into a bucket.

"Hopefully Mrs. Hutchins will let me get water from the wellhouse out back."

"Don't tell me you're going to clean the museum...?"

She nodded. "Has to be done. Father had to see the site blown up. I don't want him to see this."

"I'll come help you."

"No, Ma. The McAllisters will need help planning everything. They've still got the other three that need to be looked after, too." She kissed her mother on the top of her head and headed out.

Without looking at anyone, Elizabeth walked with her head high toward the museum. Once there, she took her broom and swept debris off the tables, then cleaned the floor. The blacking, she knew, would not come off completely. Still, she could scrape up what she could. The whitewash would scrub off with some soap and elbow grease.

But the oreodont skull...

Fighting back tears, she tied on her large apron and found an empty cigar box. Using the forceps, she deftly picked out all the shattered bone fragments and placed them with the two large chunks of the skull in the box. When she finished, she cleaned up the remaining debris and went out to dump it into the street.

Hearing footsteps on the wooden planks of the sidewalk, she looked up to see several people carrying buckets and rags coming toward her. They nodded to her and came in the door. Two of the men filled the buckets with water, before coming back in where everyone had scattered to different areas and begun work. Some busied themselves scrubbing the whitewash off the fossils and the tables and walls, while others took scrapers and tackled the blacking.

Lydia Hutchins caught her eye and winked, then went back to scrubbing the floor. Elizabeth looked around at the industry of the small representation of the town, and went to the shelf that held their chemicals, picking up the only bottle left undisturbed. It held the light glue that was used to piece bones and bone fragments together. As the townspeople worked, she began piecing the oreodont skull back together, one sliver of bone at a time.

Sometime around one, Mrs. Hutchins brought in sandwiches and apples for everyone. Mr. Hutchins brought in a pail of lemonade and mugs. He then turned to Elizabeth.

"We want you to know that most of us denounced the vandalism as barbaric. Don't let the actions of a few taint your feelings toward the rest."

She swallowed the tears that started, and nodded, not trusting her voice. After eating, everyone continued working on the rooms. Elizabeth fine-tuned the work of those toiling with fossils to prevent further harm. The blacksmith showed up for a little while to fix the door and its lock. With a nod and a hand to her shoulder, he gave her the new key.

By the time the sun began to set, the museum was in a good state compared to what it had been in. People faded away, until only she and Lydia were left. The girl hugged her as Elizabeth locked up, and disappeared into her parents' store.

Walking slowly, Elizabeth carried the bucket of dirty rags home. She could smell fried potatoes when she got close to the cabin and realized she was very hungry. Her mother had flavored the potatoes with some ham and she sniffed appreciatively.

"I went by to see if you needed some help, but saw you were about overrun with it."

"Yes, several of the townsfolk came by."

"All in all, people are good."

"It would seem so…"

She ate as though in a daze. Exhaustion pulled at her, but she forced herself to wash up and pull on a clean shift before climbing into bed, where she slept deeply until morning.

****

The morning light washed over her as she lay in her bed. The air about her face was cold, and she relished the warmth beneath the covers for a moment longer. But the day called, and she pushed the covers aside with a sigh.

Dressed in her old pink calico, she went down the stairs and heated up the leftovers from the night before. Her mother was gone already, ministering somewhere no doubt, and she ate a quiet breakfast before scattering seed and scraps to the chickens.

Fido caught another prairie dog for his breakfast and she left him to it.

Closing her eyes, she breathed in the cool, dry air and breathed out slowly. It was Thursday, and she needed to go get supplies for the crew. First up, borrow a mule from Riggs.

The mule yard was busy. Farmers were seeding pastures and it was not uncommon for a horse or mule to step in a prairie dog hole and be injured.

Andy Riggs kept several mules for hire should anyone need one, or even a team. Elizabeth waited while he settled up with one of farmers.

"Yes, miss?"

She tried to gauge his attitude toward her, but was unable to read his deadpan expression. Andy Riggs was nothing if not dour.

"Needing a mule for supplies again?"

"Yes, sir. Have you one available?"

"Got that spotted one that belonged to ol' Jim."

"Can I have him?"

"Yeah, sure. It'll cost ten cents for the day."

She dug the coin out of her pocket and handed it over while he went to untie the gray-muzzled mule.

She patted him on the neck and led him to the back of the general store, tying him securely to the post there.

The inside of the store bustled already with people from all over the region. She took her list to Lydia, who was wearing a new dress of deep blue calico.

"That's a beautiful dress, Lydia."

"Thank you, Elizabeth. I'll get these things out to the mule if you want to wait inside. Dad will lash them on for you."

"That would be wonderful."

She wandered around the store while Lydia worked in the background, hauling bags of beans and flour, cornmeal and salt out to the back.

"You'll have to go to the new butcher for meat soon."

"So I heard."

"Ol' Jenkins is so excited, he nearly sawed his finger off the other day." Lydia laughed, though Elizabeth could not feel it was a laughing matter.

Soon her goods were out on the back porch waiting to be loaded onto the mule. It was done quickly and she left the quiet industry of the store to lead the mule out to the site.

Chapter Twenty

Rock pressed against his hip as he struggled for a foothold. He lay stretched out on the gully floor, arm craned up and over as he reached into the deep crack where the skull lay. Morty was working to get the overburdening rock away from it, and he was clearing the remainder from around the back of the skull. It was uncomfortable to say the least.

In his mind, Daniel pictured Elizabeth in his place and smiled. She would have done it happily with no complaint. He would do the same.

But now the light was darkening into twilight and the dig was closing down for the day. He rolled to a sitting position, and groaned at the stiffness in his limbs. He gathered his tools together before rising to go to the fire and eat whatever Charlie had fixed for them.

It was a rabbit stew, compliments of Eddie who'd shot a brace of jackrabbits that morning. Daniel had always thought that rabbit tasted of nothing, not even gamey as range meat often was. But this stew was full of flavor, and he wondered again where Charlie had learned cooking. There were the usual teasing remarks mixed with thanks for the meal.

Then Charlie said, "We're low on some items. Do we need to go into town?"

Ingram thought. "Tomorrow is Thursday. Let's see if Elizabeth comes with some supplies. If she doesn't, we'll send a couple on Friday."

Thursday! Daniel's heart leapt at the thought that he might see Elizabeth the next day. He walked to the creek, ostensibly to wash his bowl, in order to have just a few moments alone with his thoughts about her.

A sound interrupted his thoughts.

It was unusual—pitched high and yet guttural. He froze, straining to hear through the blood pounding in his ears. His hand reached into his holster and pulled the pistol free. The last of the daylight was augmented by an early moon. He scanned the area and finally saw it—a coyote.

It staggered alongside the creek. And yet it did not drink or move toward it. It was simply coming toward him, eyes black and depthless in the twilight.

He pulled the gun up and aimed. The beast was still a distance away, far enough to make precision awkward in the dim light. He forced himself to wait a full minute as it struggled on toward him. Moonlight glinted off a string of saliva coming from its mouth.

The shot rang out and the coyote dropped, writhing, to the ground. It snarled and thrashed, though its movements became slower and finally stopped. By then, he was surrounded by the rest of the crew.

"What's going on?"

"What happened?"

"Is it the Howell crew?"

Daniel shook his head, gesturing toward the twitching coyote. "I think it was rabid."

"Hydrophoby…" one man whispered.

"Let's bury it, quick," Ingram said.

Someone left to get a shovel. Eddie grabbed the dead coyote by the hind legs and dragged it into the brush where another man was busy digging a hole. Daniel holstered his gun and ran a hand over his face. He was still sweating from the experience.

He pushed through the remaining men and headed back to the camp. How would they all sleep knowing there were rabid animals about? Someone would have to keep watch.

As the men came back, he looked at Ingram and said, "We need to set up a watch for the night."

Ingram nodded. "There's eight of us. Four a night. Two hours each. I'll start now. Daniel, I'll wake you in a couple hours. You'll wake Frank, who will wake Eddie."

The rest nodded. Daniel rolled into his blanket and laid his head down on his pack. Eyes closed, he tried to drift off, but sleep eluded him. All he could think about was that Elizabeth might be coming… and pray that she would be safe.

****

Breakfast consisted of the last of the eggs and bacon, and some flatbread to go with it. Charlie seemed to relish his position as camp cook, and Daniel, for one, was grateful for him. He wolfed down his plateful, then picked up the tools and strode to the dig site.

The men had made good work of the overburden. They had now set aside the pick-axes, and picked up the large chisels and hammers to finish the job. Daniel lay back down to reach the skull in its deep fissure through the rock. But his entire being was waiting for the call that Elizabeth had come.

The sun was high in the sky before she showed up. The old spotted mule was with her, laden with goods that the men happily divested from it. Her gaze sought him out, and she smiled broadly when she saw him.

He grinned and went up to her, stopping short of actually grabbing and lifting her in his arms. Instead, he pointed to her large apron and said, "You're planning to work."

She nodded, then the smile faded. "I need to talk to Father."

He frowned. "What happened?"

She gestured for him to follow and she went up to her father, who stopped in the middle of his tirade against Howell's crew.

"Yes, Elizabeth?"

"Father, something has happened to the museum."

His mouth dropped open, and he whispered, "What… the Fossil Emporium?"

She took a breath. "It was attacked. Many of the fossils were painted with whitewash and blacking, or thrown to the ground and broken. The oreodont skull…" She paused and her eyes glittered. "The oreodont skull was smashed. I have saved the pieces and will reassemble it, but…"

"Smashed? Defaced? Why?"

"I don't know. I thought the town was against us, but they all came together to help me clean up the mess."

Ingram shook his head.

A cold fire of rage welled up inside Daniel at the senseless attack. "Howell's crew—I'll bet you."

Elizabeth turned to him, dabbing her eyes with the edge of her apron. "They haven't been in town. I don't know who it was."

Ingram shook himself and laid a hand on her shoulder. "Well, the great thing is you are well and unharmed. Your mother… is she all right?"

"Mother is fine."

Her dog, Fido, nosed her hand and Daniel said, "I shot a rabid coyote last night. Keep an eye on your dog."

Her eyes widened and she nodded, reaching down to fondle the ears of the cur. She looked toward the dig site. "Can you show me the skull? How far have you gotten?"

He smiled down at her. "Come see. Your father says we have gotten to… I forget the word. You'll know it when you see it."

She knelt and peered at the place where he had been chipping away. "I think that's the parietal, and part of the frontal there at the farthest part. Nicely done."

A warm glow filled him at her praise and his ears grew hot. He tried to pull his hat down to cover them, but her focus was still on the fossil skull.

"Here's the beginning of the lower jaw, I'll wager." She pointed to a brown fleck in the rock.

"You think so?"

She nodded. "Hand me that chisel and hammer and we'll see…"

He gave her the tools and she chipped the stone away from the bone. Soon it had expanded and she pointed to a developing pit. "That's the surangular bone all right. We've got a lower jaw to go with our skull."

She lifted a triumphant face to him and he bent to kiss her, then realized they were surrounded by men working on the skeleton and stopped. She smiled knowingly and went back to work. He fetched another set of tools and worked from the top of the skull downward toward her. They chipped away in companionable silence for a while.

"Will you be able to piece together the oreodont skull?"

A little silence, then she said, "With enough patience and glue, yes. There will be vacuities. Some of it was just dust."

"I could strangle the man who did that."

"Careful what you say. Sheriff still wants to lock you up for murder."

"True. And I am no closer to figuring out who did it all. It isn't as though I could go waltzing into the Howell camp and ask questions now."

"No, I suppose not. What are you going to do? If you left the state…"

"I can't do that. I was released conditionally only. I may still have to face a jury."

"But you're innocent…"

"I'm glad you think so."

"Oh, Daniel… I mean, Mr. Bridger."

"I like it when you call me Daniel."

"Well, it isn't proper."

He snorted at that. "If you knew of some of the things 'proper' young ladies have done around me, you would be shocked."

"I'm shocked enough at how I've behaved."

He looked up and caught her eye. "Truly?"

Her hazel eyes stared back. "Well, perhaps that is a strong word." She stretched and rose, adding, "I need to refill my canteen."

She walked away and he could not stop himself from grinning.

He came to a tricky part where the thin strut of the

skull bone came tantalizingly close to the edge of the rock. He needed to chip around it, leaving enough matrix in place to protect the bone in transport to the museum. Time passed, and he began to wonder what was taking Elizabeth so long when a shout went up. He looked over to see Elizabeth in the arms of another man.

His first reaction was one of jealous rage, but then he saw that she was held from behind with a pistol at her head. He paused mid-step. There were other men now, all with guns pointed at Ingram's men.

Howell cocked his rifle and pointed it at the whole site. "Dr. Ingram, I am going to give you one chance to get off my site."

"This is my site, Howell, as you well know."

"I think you'll find the mayor and the sheriff agree with me."

"Why would you want a site that your men blew up? The whole thoracic section is ruined."

"But you have a nice skull and long bones. The rest of the sauropod is intact. Far better than the rotten hindquarters of a common hadrosaur."

"Put down your guns and release Elizabeth. We can talk reasonably about this."

"I'm done being reasonable. Cede the site to me and your daughter goes free."

"Father, don't!" Elizabeth shouted.

"I have no choice, Elizabeth."

A tense moment reigned and a few hammers were cocked. Daniel reached for his pistol but Howell's rifle barrel glinted in the sunlight.

"Don't, Bridger. I don't need much of an excuse to take you out."

Just then, another ring of men appeared on horseback, also with rifles. But these guns were pointed at Howell's men. Enoch Darden shifted his pistol to the head of the man holding Elizabeth hostage.

"Let her go. I've got the army at my side."

A tense moment passed. Then, the man holding Elizabeth shoved her forward and she fell amongst the rocks and brush. Daniel let loose a choked cry. He ran forward to lift her up and pull her tightly to him.

Darden wasn't finished. "Howell, you and your crew are being taken back to Denver to be held without bail."

"Mayor Janney and Sheriff Hancock—"

"Have both denounced you, when faced with possible arrest. They've given you up, Howell. You have no one to turn to."

"Who the hell are you?"

"I'm a Pinkerton detective. Our job was to infiltrate the factions and determine if the Cope-Marsh war had spread to Denver and its dinosaur fields. Even if it wasn't related to the larger hostilities, what we found was equally dangerous: men willing to maim and kill for the sake of old bones."

"But in the end, it's just your word against all of ours."

"Not just my word."

Daniel stifled the jangle of nerves that galvanized him, gently put Elizabeth aside, and stepped forward. "There's me, too."

"Bridger, you're just a drifter. Who's gonna believe you?" Howell said.

"He's a Pinkerton detective like me. We've both got a dossier full of evidence to bring Janney and Wilke down. The best you boys can do is turn state's evidence against them."

Starting with the man who had held Elizabeth captive, the Howell crew laid down their guns, though Howell was the last to do so. Daniel looked down at a wide-eyed Elizabeth, who stared back at him.

"I'm sorry I didn't tell you. I hadn't planned on finding you on this job."

"I…I don't know what to say…"

"Don't say anything, yet."

"But, was anything real?"

He reached down and pulled her into an embrace. She struggled lightly, but he put a stop to that with a single kiss. She melted against him, and hoots and shouts filled the air.

"How real do you want it to be?" he asked against her lips.

"This is a good start," she answered.

He smiled, then bent to kiss her again.

Chapter Twenty-One

"Lizzie! Elizabeth!" her mother shouted up the stairs.

"Yes, Ma?" she said in a groggy tone.

"Come eat your breakfast."

"*Mmmft*," was all she said.

Her father was already at the table. He had been up late the night before talking to the Denver detectives, and yet he was wide awake now and eating heartily. She sucked in a deep breath and sat. Her mother dished her up a plate and set it before her.

"Thanks, Ma."

"Of course. Is Mr. Bridger coming by this morning?"

"I don't know. He had to go to Denver as soon as we all got back from the site yesterday."

"I'm still not sure what happened."

Elizabeth looked to her father, but he shook his head and took another bite of bacon and potatoes. She sighed and said, "Daniel found evidence that Wilke and Janney were trying to steal Father's *Camarasaurus* site. With the murder of Silent Jim, it become serious. Then MacMillan was killed, and Daniel was blamed for that. When John caught rabies and was shot by Howell, Howell blamed Daniel for that and he was arrested."

"All right. So Daniel was put in jail for those, and you ministered to him."

"Yes. Then Enoch Darden was sent in. He investigated first with Father's crew, then went over to the Howell crew. Apparently Howell did a fair amount of bragging about what they had done. Then someone smashed up the museum…some thugs paid by Janney." Her voice faltered, but she found it again and continued. "Daniel had asked me to get a message to a Matthew Mattis, and so I sent a telegram. Mr. Mattis got a Denver lawyer to get Daniel released. He then rushed out to the site to warn us of Howell's plan to blow up the *Camarasaurus*. He arrived almost too late."

"But you were saved in time."

"All of us, but yes."

"And where is he now?"

"He has gone to Denver to report… or something."

"And in the end, who killed those men?"

"According to Enoch Darden it was Will Gunn, Janney's man."

"I never did like that man. Always hovering about…"

The table went silent. Then her father leaned back.

"I need to go back out to the site. We have to get that skull out, and with Daniel gone, there's only me."

"I could do it!"

"Yes, but your mother told me she needs you here for the next couple of days. Something about washing the quilts and oiling the wood or something…"

Elizabeth's heart fell. A skull! And lost due to laundry. And Daniel was gone for who knows how long. Her mother must have seen the look on her face for she cleared her throat.

"Well, as to that, it may rain tomorrow, so we won't need to wash the quilts just yet. You may go work on the skull."

Elizabeth jumped up and hugged her mother. "Thank you!" She grabbed her straw bonnet and her tool belt, putting them on as she took her canteen to the ewer to fill it up. Her father kissed her mother and they headed off.

She thought about Daniel as she went along. What were they going to do? Daniel had his work, and she had her bones and her parents. Both needed her, and she needed them. But she loved him, and he loved her, she knew. Could they be happy seeing each another a few times a year when one of them could travel to the other? Her heart sank, and her feet dragged for a few steps until her father called her to speed.

Fido brought her a stick which she hefted and threw it for him. He raced off through the brush and returned after a few minutes, stick in mouth. They repeated this for a while until a jackrabbit caught his attention and he darted off.

The sounds of hammers on chisels echoed off the stone walls of the gulley as they neared the site. She loosened the ribbons holding her bonnet in place and took it off. The skull was in the shade by this point in the day and she would need all the light possible to differentiate bone from rock.

Her father's pace quickened and he all but ran to the point where the skull lay partially chipped from the surrounding rock. Elizabeth followed and knelt beside it to before pulling her hammer and smaller chisel free. First, she assessed the state of the skull and the lower jaw. They were together, and had been preserved slightly agape showing a few of the spoon-shaped teeth.

She spent a little time defining the edges of the

skull while her father worked some of the overburden back. Now and then she brought out her mirror to bring in some light to define the edge of a bone.

Soon they were working their way down to pedestal out the skull so that it could be safely removed and taken back to the museum, to be completely cleared from its matrix. As she chipped and scraped, she tried not to think about Daniel, but even the excitement of a skull was unable to remove him completely from her mind.

Her cheeks warmed as she remembered their last few moments together, before he got on the stagecoach to Denver.

He had looked down at her, deep brown eyes burning into hers, and whispered, "This isn't goodbye. I'll be back."

"But for how long? I know your home is back east, and your job is wherever they send you. And I…"

"You belong here. Out in the clear air, pulling ancient bones from the ground."

She had sighed, for it was true. Would she give that up for him? Follow him wherever he was sent? Her gut clenched at the thought, though she knew she would. Still, a piece of her would be left behind…

He'd kissed her then, gently but longingly, lips moving over hers in a way that hinted of future passion.

That had been days ago, and she had not heard from him since. The greatest fear in her heart was that his feelings would cool with distance. That he would find a way to live quite happily without her.

"Elizabeth, you're slacking."

Her father's voice urged her from her stupor. She began to chip away at the stone again.

She forced herself to focus for the rest of the afternoon. As the shadows deepened, they wrapped up for the day. The men congregated around the fire pit where Charlie stood stirring a pot of something that smelled appetizing. She and her father headed back down the path toward Matson, and home.

Fido trotted at their heels, tearing off from time to time after rabbits and ground squirrels. When they reached the house, she checked on her chickens. They were roosted comfortably inside the crate and making small noises of contentment. The smell of lamb chops and onions frying met them when they opened the door.

Ingram took a deep breath and said, "My favorite! What prompted this?"

"It's the anniversary of our marriage. Twenty-five years ago you married me, much against my father's wishes."

He hugged her from behind. "I wasn't good enough for you, but neither was anyone else!"

A shadow crossed the front window and boots echoed on the wood planks of the porch. Elizabeth went to the door just as the knock sounded and threw it open. There stood Daniel. He wore town clothes—suit and waistcoat—and looked fine. She felt rather shabby in her faded, pink calico.

Nevertheless he opened his arms and gathered her to him. When she was nestled against him, he breathed deeply of her hair and let out a long sigh.

She whispered, "You're here."

"To stay."

"What?" She pushed back to look him in the eye.

"I've left Pinkerton. I am my own man now. But, I have nothing to my name except a horse and a mule.

And various tools of a bone prospector." He grinned.

"All that could come in handy, if you stayed on with us."

They looked at Ingram, who laughed and waved his hand. "Yes, yes. Daniel is most welcome."

Daniel looked down at her. "You should know my parents are well-off. I am not. My father wants me to make something of myself. Still, that was who you telegraphed when I was in jail."

"So, you're really Daniel Mattis…"

"Yes."

"That will take some getting used to."

"You will like my parents, I think."

"Will they like me? I am not some high-society woman…"

He grinned. "Truth be told, neither are they. I think they will love you, if I can ever tear you away from your bones long enough to go meet them."

"The season ends in late fall. Of course, that's when the real prep work starts."

"Say no more. I have your promise to go meet them this fall, then. We will be married from here."

Her eyebrows arched and she leaned back from him. "Oh, will we?"

"If you'll have me…and my horse and mule."

She smiled. "As long as you bring your prospecting tools!"

He laughed, then bent and kissed her. "It's a deal." He kissed her again.

In the background, her mother called out, "Supper is ready. Come eat before these chops get tough!"

"Mother, I am getting married!"

Elsie paused in lifting out the iron skillet from the

fire. Her eyes widened and she called over her shoulder, "Bones! Bones, get in here. Your daughter is getting married."

Ingram opened the back door and frowned, "What's all this?"

"Daniel and I, we're getting married."

Ingram's mouth fell open and he stared. Then, he shook himself and grinned. "Excellent, we can keep him in the family. He will come in useful in the digs!"

"Wilberforce!" Elsie was shocked.

He looked helplessly at her, "But, dear, if you had seen how he handles a chisel…"

"Never mind. Just so we are both happy to have him in the family."

Elizabeth broke into laughter, and the others joined her.

Epilogue

The sun stood bright over the little town of Matson, lighting the foothills of the Rockies with yellows and greens of summer. Daniel stood at the front of the church, with Elizabeth beside him. The town had pressed into the small building to show their support for the couple, and possibly to apologize for believing him to be a murderer. The real murderer had been tried and hanged already, but enough time had passed so it no longer cast a pall over the celebration.

Daniel looked down at Elizabeth wearing a new dress of palest, yellow poplin, edged with white lace. Her eyes looked green and her lips even darker rose than usual. Finally, the parson declared them man and wife and he could kiss her.

He claimed her lips and held them for a moment longer than appropriate before releasing her and facing the crowd. Her eyes shone, and there was a bounce in her step as they walked down the aisle to stand by the door.

One by one the townspeople shook their hands and wished them well. As a wedding present, his father had purchased a plot of land on the outskirts of town for them, and Daniel had already made headway on building their small house.

Presents had arrived all week that would help to outfit their home once it was ready. The Hutchins had brought over a cast-iron set of cookware including a Dutch oven and skillet. Riggs had brought them Silent Jim's mule and offered it for a price they could not refuse. It was now tethered on the new property, eating happily of the fresh grasses there, along with the horse and other mule.

But best of all, the *Camarasaurus* skull sat now in the museum for all to see. Elizabeth was slowly bringing it to light from its rocky coffin. The oreodont skull was partially reassembled, and looking well enough to eventually display.

Soon the congratulating was done, and they could take their spots on the next stagecoach. He had managed to pull her away from her bones for a week in Denver at one of the fancy hotels. Another gift from his parents. He gazed down at his wife. She looked up at him.

He bent once again to kiss the daughter of bones.

A word about the author…

Born and raised in the west in California and Nevada, Grace Colline now lives in the deep south. As an adult, she travelled extensively in the US and Australia where she lived for several years. In all that time, she met lots of people from all walks of life. She tries to include variety in her characters as well, and enjoys the opportunity to travel vicariously through them.

For now, she lives with her husband, two of her five children and several dogs. She teaches online biology as an adjunct professor in her spare time. In addition, she is an avid fiber artist who spins wool and other materials into yarn, and then knits it up into all manner of things.

****

gracecollinehistorical.com

****

If you enjoyed this story, leaving a review at your favorite book retailer or reader website would be much appreciated. Thank you!